Th

l

A Colonel Bainbridge Mystery

Book 1

By
Evelyn James

Red Raven Publications 2023

www.redravenpublications.com

The Gentleman Detective is the first novel in the
Colonel Bainbridge Mysteries

Other titles in the Series:
The Unholy Preacher
The Unwelcome Guests
The Last Word in Pickles
The Mayfair Mystery
Murder on ice

All available on Amazon Kindle
Coming soon in Paperback

Chapter One

Colonel Bainbridge retrieved his hat and walking cane from the prison guard.

"I imagine we shall be seeing you again soon, sir," the guard said in his jovial manner. Bainbridge recalled that his name was Mayfair, like the place in London.

"Yes, probably," he declared bluffly, without really heeding the question.

He walked to the big prison doors which were opened by another guard and stepped out into glorious sunshine, the last dregs of a late summer's day. He lifted his chin to the sky and allowed the sun to warm his skin. It felt good to be outside again, smelling the fresh breeze and contemplating what to do next.

He was startled by the abrasive hoot of a car horn. Jolted from his daydreaming, Bainbridge looked around for the source of the sound.

"Hallo!" a voice called, followed by a whistle.

Bainbridge became aware of a woman in one of those new-fangled cars everyone of a certain age was raving about. He paused and took a closer look. The woman was

1

most certainly addressing him, but at that distance, and without his glasses on, he was not sure who she was. Who, in fact, would be coming to meet him as he left the prison?

Curiosity overrode Bainbridge's natural caution and he wandered over to see who this strange lady was. As he came closer, he could see she was wearing a green dress and driving goggles, while her straw hat was firmly clamped down on her head by means of a flimsy, white silk scarf tied beneath the chin. The car engine was rumbling in that puttering, muttering fashion car engines did, occasionally giving out a percussive blast like a consumptive having a good cough.

"Hallo Uncle!"

"Good heavens, Victoria!"

Bainbridge stared up at his niece perched high on a black leather seat, one hand cautiously attached to the steering wheel.

"When did you get a car?"

"Oh, just recently," Victoria replied gleefully. "Technically it was Sven's, but he gifted it to me. Do climb up."

Bainbridge assessed the motorised wagon for means to climb onto it and identified a footrest that looked suitable for the purpose. Bainbridge had once been a first-class boxer, along with a jolly good horseman (he had been in the cavalry after all). He had prided himself on his strong physique, but age had caught up with him and his chest muscles seemed to have slumped to around his belly area, at least this was his excuse for his growing girth.

Houston had teased him about it, but then Houston had been no spring chicken himself. In the end, that had done for him.

"Who is Sven?" Bainbridge asked as he struggled into the passenger seat beside Victoria.

"Oh, we were going to be married," she carried on conversationally. "Until I discovered he was also seeing that slip of a thing who teaches the Tuttle children. I called the whole thing off, but I kept the car."

2

Victoria set the car rolling forward at a comfortable walking pass. An elderly man on a Penny Farthing, passed them easily, doffing his hat politely to them.

"What are you doing here?" Bainbridge asked. "I haven't seen you since, since…"

"Christmas 1897," Victoria replied promptly.

"That long?" Bainbridge gasped, he could have sworn it was far more recent, where did time go?

"I am so sorry I haven't been to see you," Victoria continued. "I wanted to come, but mother…"

"Yes, your mother's feelings towards me are legendary," Bainbridge sighed at mention of his younger sister. Ten years his junior, he had always been fond of her, but as she grew older, she first found him an embarrassment, then became ashamed of him, until finally she deemed him too appalling to have anything to do with. It would not be so bad if Bainbridge had actually done something really terrible, he could understand it then. It just seemed his sister was horrified by his manners and choice of friends.

"How are you here now?" Bainbridge asked.

"Well, we saw in the paper about Houston and I said I had to call on you and see how you were doing. Mother protested, of course…"

"Of course."

"…but as I had the car, I didn't have to listen to her."

Victoria patted the car's steering wheel with a smile.

"You know, I was thinking that marrying Sven would give me freedom from Mother, it turns out all I needed was a car."

She fell silent.

"I am very sorry about Houston."

Colonel Bainbridge took a deep breath. Every time he thought about Houston, his dearest friend, and the man he could always rely on, a tight, painful knot developed in his chest and it felt a little like he was dying too. Sometimes he was not sure he was going to be able to carry on without him at his side. He felt as if a part of him was missing.

"It was a shock."

"I should say. The papers said he was shot by a man during a bank robbery?"

"It was something like that," Bainbridge swallowed down on his pain. "Can we not talk about it?"

They drove for a while in silence.

"How did you know I was at the prison?" Bainbridge asked.

"Your housekeeper. She said you would probably appreciate a lift. She seemed quite concerned about you."

"Mrs Huggins is an old fusspot," Bainbridge said moodily, though not without a hint of affection for the woman who had cooked him his meals and kept his house for the last twenty-five years.

"When she said the prison, I thought she meant you were serving a sentence!" Victoria chuckled, a smidge of anxiety in her tone.

"Heavens no!" Bainbridge responded. "I was only visiting someone. Not everyone who finds themselves on the wrong side of the law is truly a criminal, my dear. Sometimes it just comes down to very bad timing."

The car turned onto a main thoroughfare and they slowly passed by a department store.

"What are you going to do now?" Victoria asked him.

"How do you mean?" Bainbridge frowned.

"The detective agency. I mean, without Houston…"

"Are you suggesting I am not an adequate detective on my own?" Bainbridge huffed, deeply insulted.

"I would never suggest that," Victoria said. "I just thought that Houston was the driving force and without him you might retire."

"Retire?" Bainbridge spluttered the word which had, in truth, been bandied about by Mrs Huggins recently too. Especially after Houston took three bullets to the chest and died before an ambulance could reach him. And Houston had been younger than him… "I wouldn't know what to do with myself."

"Oh," Victoria said, pausing before adding. "You know,

if you did retire, mother might mellow a bit. It was always the detective business she found so distasteful."

"I don't need your mother's approval," Bainbridge sniffed haughtily. "If she can't accept me for who I am, so be it."

Victoria wisely did not press the matter.

They were close to Bainbridge's home, a nice early Victorian denizen set back from the road and surrounded by a fine garden that Bainbridge always failed to enjoy as much as he intended to. A white wall marked the boundaries and they headed through an entrance flanked by two tall white pillars and an open pair of black iron gates. Bainbridge rarely shut them. He had always wanted his home to be welcoming to whoever needed him. Some desperate souls had come to him and Houston over the years, plodding their way to his door to seek assistance in times of dire straits. He had never turned anyone away.

Victoria negotiated the car through the gates and up the short drive, coming to a halt with only a slight jerk before a white, pillared portico.

"You are home," Victoria informed him needlessly.

"Not until I clamber off this thing," Bainbridge muttered, edging himself to the side of his seat and leaning out a foot cautiously. He found the footrest and lowered himself down with great care.

Victoria was slapping dust from her dress and waiting for him. He wondered why she was still here, considering her mother must be having kittens at her absence. He hoped she would go soon. He wanted to be alone. He had a lot of thinking to do, and a lot of grieving.

He wandered up to his front door and opened it, he hesitated a moment then glanced at Victoria who seemed inclined to follow him indoors. There was a cheerful smile on her face.

"Will your mother be worried?" he hinted.

"I really could not say," Victoria said in a voice that said she knew exactly how worried her mother would be and did not care.

Bainbridge's sister had that effect on people.

"Well, I won't keep you," Bainbridge said, edging himself inside, thinking she just wanted to make sure he was safely indoors.

But no, Victoria followed him, and if he tried to block the door it would look as if he were being deliberately rude, and Bainbridge was never that, so he allowed her in.

Victoria glanced around his front hall.

"Why, it hasn't changed a bit!" she declared.

Bainbridge looked around sheepishly.

"Has it not? Houston did keep saying about a lick of paint…"

Bainbridge tailed off as he remembered his dead friend. A fresh wave of sombreness came over him at the thought. He wasn't sure he was ever going to get used to Houston being gone. He was not even sure he wanted to get used to it.

Lost in thought he wandered into his favourite room, the front drawing room which caught the sun all day. He spent more hours in here than anywhere else.

Victoria followed. She paused before a small octagonal table that displayed photographs in silver frames. At the front was the most recent picture. Victoria picked it up.

Bainbridge did not need to look at it to know the image, it was ingrained on his mind. It had been their last case together. They had solved a fire insurance scandal, finding out that a seeming victim of arson was, in reality, the arsonist. They had been praised by the insurance firm who had hired them and who they had saved from paying out a small fortune. The company had insisted on taking a photograph of the Gentlemen Detectives, stood on the steps of the insurance building. Later the image had been in all the newspapers.

Houston had insisted they obtain a copy and frame it. He said it would be good publicity, Bainbridge told him it was vanity. Houston replied he was only saying that because Bainbridge did not like how he looked in the picture, and he was getting a copy anyway.

Funny how such a casual incident stuck in the mind. It was the last photo he had of Houston. The last ever photo, unless you counted that hideous one some ghastly journalist had snapped at the scene of the robbery. The picture of Houston crumpled on the ground had been in the evening papers and had been stuck in Bainbridge's mind ever since.

Victoria put the picture down without comment. For that Bainbridge was grateful.

"I always loved this room," Victoria said. "The sun falls beautifully into it."

"It does," Bainbridge agreed.

"And do you still have that spare bedroom right above here?" Victoria asked.

"I do," Bainbridge said. "Can't think the last time it was used."

"Oh good," Victoria said with a sigh of relief.

Bainbridge glanced her way, there was something in her manner.

"Victoria?"

"Uncle, you must not be angry, nor must you protest, for I shall not be deterred," Victoria said in a breathless race to get out the words. "I have made a decision and I shall stick by it, no matter what."

"Oh dear, what have you done?" Bainbridge asked, foreseeing a future where his sister would hate him even more than she already did. He could almost feel her ire pouring out towards him already, as if he had somehow influenced Victoria into doing whatever this thing was.

He was a co-conspirator in the matter now. An unwitting one, but that would not matter to his sister.

"Well?" he asked Victoria.

"It's really all rather silly," Victoria said, trying to soften the news. "Mother lost her head a little when I broke off the engagement with Sven and we have been barely talking ever since. Seeing the newspapers about Houston, and Mother refusing to let me come and see you, was the last straw. I cannot stand it any longer Uncle. I feel a prisoner in my own home. So, I decided I was not going to stand for it anymore!"

"You have runaway, haven't you?" Bainbridge groaned.

"I prefer to consider this a bold step towards my personal emancipation, along with striking a chord with all girls suffering under the tyranny of an oppressive parent," Victoria said in a voice that sounded like she was rousing the troops for war, then she lowered her voice. "But yes, in essence, I have runaway."

"And you came here," Bainbridge said solemnly.

"Where else could I go?" Victoria said, anxious now. "You won't turn me away?"

Bainbridge looked into her worried face and felt a small pang of satisfaction that his niece had proven herself to be a little more like him than his sister would care for.

"I never turn anyone away," he said.

"Thank goodness!" Victoria gasped.

"The spare bedroom is all yours, but I will insist you write to your mother directly, so she knows you are safe and well."

Victoria gave a small snort at this information, then nodded her head.

"Agreed."

"Good," Bainbridge leaned back in his chair and his head sagged a little. It had been a long and emotionally taxing day. Tomorrow looked likely to be the same. Maybe this would be how it always was from now on?

"Uncle, can I ask something?" Victoria asked.

Bainbridge lifted his head.

"I would prefer you to call me Julius if you intend staying here. I have always found the title 'uncle' makes me feel rather old."

"Julius," Victoria corrected herself, getting her tongue used to the name. "Very well, but can I ask you something?"

"It is about Houston, isn't it?"

"Yes."

Bainbridge found his eyes straying to the picture frame

on the table, the one where he and Houston were stood side by side outside the insurance building. Houston was grinning at the camera, proud of the moment, while Bainbridge seemed to be scowling. The photograph had caught him out, he had not been ready. He hated having his picture taken, anyway. If he had only known that would be his last picture with Houston, he would have smiled.

"Go on then," he declared. "But I might not answer."

Victoria accepted this.

"Are you investigating his murder?"

Bainbridge felt as if ice had formed in his chest and his heart had skipped a beat. His voice was gruff when he replied.

"Of course I am investigating it."

Chapter Two

Colonel Bainbridge assisted his niece in settling in. She had managed to stash a small valise in the back of the car, demonstrating to her doubtful uncle how a compartment behind the seats opened for storage. Once she was in the spare room and happily unpacking, Bainbridge wandered back downstairs to speak to Mrs Huggins.

"Come to stay? For how long?" the anxious housekeeper demanded.

"For as long as she wishes," Bainbridge explained.

The housekeeper looked despondent at the news. She was not used to having young ladies in the house. She glanced around the kitchen and wrung her hands together.

"I am sure she will be very accommodating," Bainbridge promised her. "It is only temporary."

Of that, at least, he was hopeful. His sister had many faults, but she could not surely have completely alienated her only child as to result in a permanent estrangement.

"Just as long as she knows I don't do the laundry. Not with my arthritis," Mrs Huggins said.

"I shall make her aware that a girl comes in weekly to deal with the washing," Bainbridge patted her arm vaguely, she seemed to need consoling. "It will be alright."

Having thoroughly upset his housekeeper, Bainbridge retreated to the drawing room to return to moping about the death of his detective partner. Victoria's direct question about whether he was investigating his friend's demise had hit a nerve. He had declared he was investigating and that was true enough, he had made discreet enquiries. The problem was he found himself stumped before he started. He had no idea why Houston was at the bank that day, and why, despite there being numerous people in the place at the time of the robbery, and several shots being fired, only Houston was hit. Three times. In the chest.

Houston had not said he was going to the bank. He had said he was going for a walk. They were still recovering from the fire insurance case and were both a touch jaded. It was always the way after the hype and adrenaline of a case. You worked day and night, taking irregular meals and even more irregular sleep. You didn't stop because you were too fired up and then it was over, and all that exhaustion caught up with you. It seemed to be getting worse the older they got too, at least it seemed worse to Bainbridge.

Houston had still been having trouble sleeping, while Bainbridge was catnapping all over the place in a desperate effort to shake off his fatigue. When Houston had said he was going for a walk, Bainbridge had been dozing in his comfy armchair and had given a muffled response before slipping into pleasant, peaceful dreams.

It was much later when the frantic ringing of the doorbell roused him, and he was told the terrible news. He still could not help thinking he should have made the effort to say a proper goodbye. He had simply taken for granted that Houston would return for dinner. It had never crossed his mind he would be gone for good.

"Why were you at the bank, Houston? It wasn't even

your bank."

Bainbridge had searched through Houston's office at the house, he had looked for some clue, but if his partner was conducting an investigation he was unaware of, he had kept it well hidden. There was nothing to tell him what had been going on.

The colonel was distracted by the ringing of the doorbell. Lately that innocuous sound had taken on an aura of dread for him and he found himself quite unable to rise and answer it, despite the person pulling quite vigorously on the bell pull.

As it happened, Victoria was coming down the stairs and answered it herself.

"Hello?"

"Bainbridge about?" a familiar voice asked.

Bainbridge knew at once who his visitor was.

"Come in Mr Flint."

Mr Flint was a short swarthy fellow who rolled like he was perpetually aboard a ship. He had, indeed, been a seaman in his former life, before forsaking the ocean to open a pub in the decidedly inland city of Norwich. That was how he had first come across Bainbridge and Houston, who liked to spend their Sunday afternoons over a pint of beer and had found The Sailor's Arms tucked in a corner of Elm Hill.

Bainbridge mournfully wondered who he would spend his Sunday afternoons with now. He hated Sundays, on the principal that nothing ever happened on them.

"What has happened Mr Flint?"

Mr Flint had a look of deep concern on his chestnut brown face. Wrinkles that were deep enough to hide a pencil folded around the bridge of his nose and concertinaed his forehead.

"It's the boy again, Colonel. And this time he has really dropped himself in it."

Bainbridge noted that Victoria was hovering in the doorway, he was about to mention she should leave them to discuss things privately, when Mr Flint burst out into a lengthy monologue of his woes.

"They have arrested him for murder, Colonel Bainbridge, and you and I both know he ain't capable of that! He was off carousing last night and he got himself into bother with some other lads. He came back bruised and bloodied, took the worst of it I would say, and serves him right. He couldn't make any sense and I sent him off to bed to sleep off the worst. Then this morning the police came knocking at my door. I didn't want to let them in, Colonel, I remember what you said about they can't be bothering me for no reason. But they insisted and there was nothing I could do. Said the boy had done for a man and he was going to swing for it."

"Take a breath, Mr Flint," Bainbridge instructed firmly. "This calls for a cool head. Now, I am assuming Franklin is denying all knowledge of the crime?"

"He is, Colonel, Sir. He says he knows nothing about it and that he was the one nearly killed last night. But the police say there are witnesses, Sir. Witnesses!"

"Don't get too alarmed about that. Witnesses are a questionable force," Bainbridge said firmly. "More than likely, the real murderer is among them and they are covering for him."

"You think so, Colonel?" Flint asked with pathetic desperation. "The boy isn't bad at heart, you know, a little wayward, but what can you expect considering how he was raised?"

"And you have given him a fine home and good employment, Mr Flint," Bainbridge agreed. "Your faith in Franklin speaks volumes. Have the police taken him to the cells?"

"They have, Sir. Just now. As soon as they were gone, I legged it over here. I knew you would help me Colonel, I knew it. You and Mr Fairchild have always watched out for me. I was so sorry to hear the news about him, Sir, dreadfully sorry. That was no way for a good fellow like him to go."

"No, it wasn't," Bainbridge said solemnly, before

remembering himself. "I shall go to see Franklin at once."

"Thank you, Sir. I shall have your pint waiting for you on Sunday, never fear."

Mr Flint tugged at his forelock, a rather landlubber gesture for a former seaman, but he did not have a hat to doff and demonstrate his respect, he had rushed out of the pub and forgot it. He slipped past Victoria, barely noticing her, and let himself out.

"Well," Victoria said, after he was gone. "I see now why Mother says you have questionable acquaintances."

"Mr Flint is a good fellow," Bainbridge said. He had risen and was searching his drawer for his trusty notebook and pen. "Your Mother fails to appreciate that it is not the outward appearance that marks a person as good or bad, but their inward inclinations. Mr Flint is generous and kindly, both traits I see rarely among the 'friends' your Mother likes to keep."

"Your point is made," Victoria said, blushing a fraction. "I was far too quick to judge. A fault I have noticed and abhorred in my Mother, yet which I have readily taken up, I fear."

She had dipped her head, looking abashed at her behaviour. Bainbridge, who had been fired up when he spoke, now realised he had been harsh and softened.

"You have plenty of time to break bad habits," he said. "Especially now you recognise them."

Victoria brightened.

"Does that mean I can come with you?"

"What?"

"To the police station. I have always wanted to see you in action. How fascinating it must be to investigate a mystery and solve it before anyone else."

"I am not sure…" Bainbridge said, visions of the horror on his sister's face were she to know he had taken his niece to a police station, dancing before his eyes. Their relationship might actually be irredeemable after that.

"You cannot possibly walk there," Victoria said firmly. "I am certain it is about to rain. In fact, I was coming downstairs to put up the roof on the car."

Bainbridge looked out at a perfectly cloudless blue sky.

"I'll have you know, Houston and I have walked miles and miles around this city and the countryside," he said with an air of injured pride.

"Then it seems to me, now is the time you took a rest from walking and came in my car. You are not getting any younger, after all, Uncle."

Bainbridge blustered at this remark, but Victoria was already in the hallway donning her driving hat and goggles. The colonel knew how this was going to go, he had seen a similar air of determination on his sister's face (though usually that was concerned with getting rid of him, not going somewhere with him). He toyed with fighting the inevitable then decided he would actually prefer to have company on his travels. He joined her at the car.

Contrary to what Victoria had said concerning rain, she was not making any attempt to pull up the car's roof. She did, however, pull on driving gloves.

"Climb aboard, Uncle."

"I thought we agreed you would call me Julius?" Bainbridge puttered as he climbed up into the car yet again. He knew he was as graceful as a beetle that has been knocked onto its back, and there was a good deal of puffing and grunting before he was installed in the passenger seat. "Why do they make these things so tall?"

"The engine has to fit," Victoria said blithely. "And if I am to call you Julius, you must call me Vicky. All my friends do."

Bainbridge adjust his girth to try to make himself comfortable.

"Vicky," he muttered.

"Julius," Victoria responded, then she pressed down the accelerator and the car jerked into a steady little roll. Any slower and it would have been in danger of being overtaken by a snail.

They exited the drive and headed in the direction

Bainbridge instructed his niece.

"So, who is Franklin?" Victoria asked as they travelled.

"He is employed as Mr Flint's potboy and general dogsbody. He had an unfortunate start to life, being sold to a freak show as a child on account of him having additional fingers and toes."

Victoria considered this information.

"How did he escape the show?"

"He wasn't drawing the crowds," Bainbridge elaborated. "Turns out having additional digits is not a crowd pleaser. The freak show was glad to be rid of him. He was on the streets a while, until Mr Flint spotted him and offered him work. That is what Mr Flint is like. He sees a soul in need, and he asks himself 'how can I help them?'."

"He does sound a very kind man," Victoria agreed. "His description of Franklin implied he was prone to violence?"

"He gets into trouble," Bainbridge agreed. "Usually someone else begins it by mocking his extra fingers. He is very sensitive on the subject. He once tried to chop them off, you know. Mr Flint had a terrible time of it. Poor fellow could not be allowed around knives for months. Thankfully, he is now more resigned to his appearance and simply restricts himself to occasionally punching a fellow's lights out for making a rude comment."

"Then, he could have killed this dead man?" Victoria pressed him. "Lost his temper and gone too far?"

"I am not inclined to believe that," Bainbridge shook his head. "It would be accidental at the worst. Franklin is a rather weak puncher. Funny when he has those extra fingers, but he lays blows softer than lamb's wool. Honestly, I cannot believe he has killed a man."

Victoria was silent and he sensed she was not so sure. Bainbridge wished he could explain his instinct for Franklin, his certainty that despite it all the poor lad was not a killer. It was hard to articulate to another person such a belief. Houston always said it was because they had met real cold-hearted killers and could tell the difference between them and normal folks. Bainbridge liked to believe that, but he also remembered his time in the army and watching lads that were as meek as mice slaughtering their enemies when the bloodlust came over them.

He felt you could never really know someone, not truly. You never knew how far they would go if pushed hard enough. Yet, contrary to that cynical perspective, he was utterly convinced that Franklin was innocent of murder, even before he had heard his story.

So maybe Houston had been right all along.

"What happens if Franklin did do it?" Victoria asked.

"What do you mean?" Bainbridge responded, shocked at the question.

"What if he did kill a man? What will you do then?"

Bainbridge could not believe she would ask something so preposterous.

"He couldn't have killed anyone," he said firmly.

"Because you promised Mr Flint that? Or because you cannot face the possibility of being wrong?"

"Vicky!"

"I have to ask. You seem to have made up your mind before we know the facts. I read the latest Sherlock Holmes, and in that…"

"I refuse to hear the wisdom of a detective in a novel," Bainbridge snorted. "That is nothing like real life."

Victoria pursed her lips with a look that was altogether too much like her mother. Bainbridge wanted to shudder.

"My point is, surely a great detective does not come to a conclusion before hearing all the facts? He does not suppose a man either guilty or innocent, until he has proof."

Bainbridge opened his mouth, wanting to stutter something out, then realised she had a point.

"Oh dear," he said instead.

"It is alright, I am sure you would have remembered that soon enough," Victoria told him consolingly. "You have just been under a lot of strain of late. That is why it is a good thing I came along."

Bainbridge glanced up as the police station came into

sight and Victoria's words sunk in.

"Oh dear," he repeated.

Chapter Three

"Good morning, Colonel," the desk sergeant greeted Bainbridge in a jolly tone.

"Good morning, Greaves," Bainbridge responded. "How is your wife?"

"Very well, Sir, very well. She wishes me to pass on her deepest condolences concerning the unfortunate Mr Fairchild, Sir. That goes for me too."

"Thank you, Greaves," Bainbridge said, moving on the subject swiftly so they did not dwell on his late friend. "I believe you are holding Franklin Ward?"

"Oh dear, yes, Sir," Greaves nodded solemnly. "Got himself in a right pickle that one. Arrested just about an hour ago for killing a man in a fist fight. Quite a shame but was bound to happen one of these days. He was always in trouble."

"Yes, yes," Bainbridge muttered, not wanting to get side-tracked into a discussion on Franklin's less distinguished qualities. "Can I see him?"

"Mr Flint sent for you, I imagine?" Greaves the desk sergeant said. "No harm in it as far as I see. The Inspector won't be fussed. He has bigger concerns on his plate with this bank robbery business…"

Greaves realised what he had said too late and swallowed hard.

"Don't concern yourself Greaves. It shall be in the papers for days, no doubt, I shall get used to it," Bainbridge let him off the hook.

"Yes, Sir. Sorry, Sir. The Inspector is looking into Mr Fairchild's murder too, Sir. Top of his list it is, honest, Sir."

"Greaves, it is really alright."

Greaves relaxed just a fraction, though not so he stopped looking like a rather awkward rabbit caught in the light of a poacher's lamp. His attention finally swivelled to Victoria.

"Can I help you, Miss?"

"I am with him," Victoria pointed a gloved finger to Bainbridge.

Greaves was confused by this new information and opened his mouth to protest.

"She is my niece, Greaves," Bainbridge said before the desk sergeant could come to any other conclusion. A policeman's mind ran in funny and often insalubrious directions.

"You have a niece, Sir?"

"These last twenty years, in fact," Bainbridge assured him.

"I am watching over Uncle Julius, to make sure he is well cared for during this difficult time," Victoria added in the sort of condescending tone best used by hospital matrons when they consider their charges to be behaving in a fashion unbecoming to swift healing.

Bainbridge looked at her in astonishment. He nearly spluttered out that he did not need taking care of by anyone, but the statement had had the appropriate effect on Greaves. Instead of looking suspiciously at Victoria and wondering about her intentions, he had softened into an expression of shared concern for the colonel.

"That is very good, Miss. My wife will be most

reassured to hear that. She has been most worried ever since we had the news about Mr Fairchild. She was even talking of going to the Colonel's house herself to make sure he was eating and so forth."

"Mr Fairchild quite watched out for my uncle," Victoria nodded.

Bainbridge was nearly choking on his stifled outrage.

"Mr Fairchild was a good egg," Greaves said, giving a slight sniff as if emotion was starting to overwhelm him. "Even with him being American, and all. I always thought as long as he was around the Colonel was in safe hands. I honestly was stunned it was Mr Fairchild who got shot, I mean if any of them were to…"

Greaves recalled that Bainbridge was stood by his shoulder and the words came to a shuddering halt. He turned towards the colonel who had turned an unattractive shade of scarlet.

"That is how it is, is it? I see now how I am thought of."

"Not at all, Colonel," Greaves said with haste. "But Mr Fairchild was a Pinkerton, wasn't he? He was a trained professional."

Bainbridge nearly exploded, but for the sake of good future relations with the police he instead stormed off down the corridor he knew so well, heading for the cells. Victoria shrugged at Greaves and then hastened to follow.

Bainbridge ignored the sound of her footsteps behind him and did not slow his pace. Despite this she caught him up easily and was not even breathless. In contrast, Bainbridge was puffing hard, partly because of his utter fury over what had just occurred.

"I'm sure he didn't mean it," Victoria said.

"He meant every word, and what about you?"

"I had to explain my presence."

"Bah!" Bainbridge snapped. "You are all against me."

"I am not," Victoria insisted.

"Everyone thinks I should retire, that I can't cope without Houston!" Bainbridge threw up his arms. "And what, I ask you, ought I to do with my time if I do retire?

21

Take up gardening?"

"I never suggested that," Victoria reminded him. "Anyway, we are here for Franklin, aren't we?"

She was distracting him. He had figured out her game. But being irate for too long gave Bainbridge a headache and he was already mellowing to his usual grumpy, grumbling self.

"Very well," he told her. "But no more telling people you are here to look after me as if I am an invalid."

"I promise," Victoria placed a hand over her heart, solemnly.

Bainbridge did not believe a word, but he knew he wasn't going to get rid of her, so he put up with her insincerity.

"Fine, fine," he turned down another corridor and they found themselves in the cells.

"How do we know which one he is in?" Victoria asked, looking at the solid iron doors.

Bainbridge ignored her and began opening the observation window on each door until he spotted Franklin.

"Franklin?" Bainbridge called into a cell when he recognised someone lying down on a hard wooden bed.

"Colonel Bainbridge!" a voice responded.

Victoria hurried alongside her uncle and looked into the cell. She saw a tall, lanky man rising from the bed where he had been laying. He was forty, if he was a day.

"I thought Mr Flint called him a boy?" Victoria whispered to her uncle.

"It is a relative term," Bainbridge replied. "He is a boy in comparison to Mr Flint."

Franklin Ward had an elongated body, as if someone had snapped pliers around his head and feet and pulled. Even his face seemed longer than it should, and all his features had a droopiness to them. Victoria presumed his curious appearance was part of the same complaint that had caused him to be born with extra fingers and toes. She had read books about the latest understanding of medical conditions, including birth defects (always while her mother was unaware) and had a vague understanding it was all due to the way the baby was formed in the womb. Possibly bad influences were involved, such as the mother taking a fright at some point in the pregnancy.

Victoria's scientific curiosity had not always led her to the most reliable of sources when it came to reading material.

"I didn't do it, Colonel," Franklin came towards the observation window and had to duck to look through. "I never killed anyone."

"What precisely happened, Franklin?" Bainbridge asked him calmly.

"I don't rightly remember. I took a few wallops myself," Franklin touched his temple where a sizeable bruise proved this statement.

"Let's start with where you went last night," Bainbridge suggested.

"I went to The Toby Jug," Franklin replied easily.

Bainbridge sighed.

"Why would you go there, Franklin? You know the sorts that go there, and they always start trouble."

"The landlady makes her own fudge. I like fudge and if I do a bit of sweeping for her, she lets me have some for free," Franklin explained. He glanced at Victoria. "Who is the lady, Colonel?"

"My niece, Victoria Bovington," Bainbridge said quickly before Victoria could introduce herself. "She was visiting when I received news of your arrest from Mr Flint."

"It's good to know someone is looking after the Colonel," Franklin nodded his long, horse-like head at Victoria. "We have all been rather worried."

"I do not need looking after," Bainbridge blustered. "I am perfectly fine. Everyone seems to think I am falling apart, either mentally or physically. I assure you I am not. I was in the cavalry for goodness sake!"

This outburst appeared to have sailed over Franklin's

tall head.

"Mr Fairchild was a Pinkerton, Miss Bovington. Did you know that? He gave it up though to come to England."

"I had heard," Victoria said uneasily. "But I think, Franklin, you ought to concentrate on answering Colonel Bainbridge's questions so we can try to get you out of this mess."

Franklin's rather rattled mind seemed to come together again at this, and he was reminded of where he was and his perilous circumstances. Terror first, then despair, crossed his features and he turned to Bainbridge.

"I have to get out of here, Colonel. I never killed anyone."

"Alright Franklin, let us be calm," Bainbridge had recovered his composure too. "You went to The Toby Jug."

"Yes. I swept the floor for a bit, then I had some fudge, and then I had a pint."

"How many pints?" Bainbridge asked.

Franklin's shrug at the query told all.

"What happened next?"

"Lots of things," Franklin said, looking confused. "Do you want to know everything?"

"I mean," Bainbridge said, corralling his patience in the face of Franklin's literalness, "how did you end up in a fight?"

"Oh," Franklin understood at last. "Simon One-Foot walked in. You know, the street boxer?"

"I recall the individual," Bainbridge said with distaste. "I have seen some of the results of his illegal matches."

"He was with some of his mates and they came to the bar. The landlady said he was barred, and he knew it. One-Foot just grinned at her and told her to draw him a pint. She was looking so upset that I got involved."

"It would have been better to call the police," Bainbridge sighed.

Franklin shrugged his shoulders again.

"I said to One-Foot we were all just having a quiet drink and he could go elsewhere. He gave me this nasty look and then he noticed my hands," Franklin took in a shuddery breath as the memory returned vividly. "He says to me, 'what is a six-fingered freak doing talking to me?' I said it takes a freak to know a freak. You know I can't hold my temper when they go on about my fingers."

Franklin was looking distraught, desperate for Bainbridge's understanding.

"I know, Franklin, I know. And that's how the fight began?"

"Not precisely," Franklin scratched his head with his right hand, giving Victoria a good glimpse of his extra finger. She tried not to stare. "The landlady insisted we were not to fight in the pub and a lot of the regulars were looking ready to back her up. One-Foot glanced about him and finally decided a dozen against him and his mates was not great odds. Jimmy Black was there, as well, and you know Jimmy is mean when his peace is disturbed."

Victoria glanced at her uncle for explanation. Bainbridge tried not to be frustrated at the interruption.

"Jimmy Black is a criminal, though you shall not find him directly involved in anything illegal. He has people for that. He is also quite nasty and quick with a cutthroat razor."

"Even Simon One-Foot knows better than to mess with Jimmy," Franklin said seriously. "Anyway, One-Foot got the message and left. Not that he liked it much."

"I don't suppose he did," Bainbridge remarked. "Stings a man like One-Foot's pride to have to back down from a fight. But if he left, how did you end up in a fight with him?"

"That is simple, Colonel," Franklin shrugged. "He waited for me. Waited two hours and when I came out of The Toby Jug, a little worse for wear, he and his mates jumped me."

"How despicable!" Victoria exclaimed. "And utterly unsporting."

"Oh, they didn't beat me up," Franklin added quickly. "They dragged me to the middle of the street and formed a circle, the three of them, around me. Then One-Foot stepped towards me and put up his fists."

"They were after a boxing match," Bainbridge groaned.

"That's it," Franklin agreed. "They were all jeering me. Calling me a six-fingered bastard, so I got all riled up and put up my fists too."

Bainbridge had a vision of the scene; the drunken Franklin, the grinning street fighter who knew he was going to win, his jeering mates egging them on. Poor Franklin with his weakling fists stood not a chance. One-Foot intended to splatter him on the ground.

"Dare I ask, what happened next?" Bainbridge said, feeling a sense of inevitability.

Franklin sniffed.

"I don't remember much," he touched his bruised temple. "I would have sworn I never laid a punch on him, but I don't know. Seems to me he battered me around the head with two hot irons. Next I knew, I woke up in the gutter. My head was spinning and felt like I had been through a mangle. Someone had gone through all my pockets and my money was gone. I felt sick as a parrot. Somehow, I got to my feet and walked home.

"Mr Flint opened the door for me and helped me in. I could barely stand up, Colonel, I was in a right bad way. I felt as though I was done for. My ears are still ringing from it."

"And you know nothing about anyone dying?" Bainbridge asked carefully.

"Not until the police came to the pub and said I had killed a man and was to be arrested," Franklin sniffed again, harder this time. "The look on Mr Flint's face, it broke my heart. I have done him wrong, Colonel, done him really wrong."

"Not if you are innocent," Bainbridge reminded him.

"They said there were witnesses," Franklin seemed defeated. "How can there be witnesses? I never killed anyone."

"That is what I am endeavouring to discover," Bainbridge assured him. "Now calm down, we have to be logical about this. You are certain you recall nothing after your fight with One-Foot except waking up in the gutter?"

"I am utterly certain," Franklin said miserably. "I sit here mulling it over. I've tried Colonel, I've tried."

"Franklin be calm I said. It is good you remember nothing except waking in the gutter, don't you see? An innocent man who had just been beaten to the ground can't remember a murder he did not commit."

A ray of hope seemed to spin down on Franklin and his face lifted in understanding.

"If that is true, Colonel, oh if that is true!"

"I shall find the truth," Bainbridge promised. "And rest assured Mr Flint is on your side. He believes you are innocent too."

Franklin's eyes filled with tears.

"That has to be the best news I've had all day," he said. "The best news."

"Our first port of call will be Mr One-Foot, to discover what he recalls of the evening."

"Oh Colonel," Franklin's face fell once again. "You don't know?"

Bainbridge felt a rumble of unease in his belly.

"Know what?"

"Simon One-Foot, Colonel. It's him they say I killed."

Chapter Four

"Damn," Colonel Bainbridge said as they walked away from the cells, then he remembered himself. "Excuse my language, Vicky."

"Under the circumstances, I fully understand," Vicky reassured him. "Do you believe Franklin?"

"Every word," Bainbridge sighed. "Which does not help us one bit. I need to speak to Inspector Dougal about this."

They returned to the front desk where Greaves nodded to them

"Any luck?"

"I need to speak to the inspector, Greaves, at once."

Greaves nodded again.

"I've already sent him a message, you just need to go upstairs to his office," he said.

"Thank you," Bainbridge replied and then he led Vicky to the stairs. "I have worked with the inspector for a number of years now. He is reliable, however, I must warn you that he has a degree of eccentricity."

"A degree in?"

"No, of," Bainbridge corrected her, before

contemplating what she had said. "Though your suggestion is not so far-fetched.

They arrived at a brown door which Bainbridge knew very well, and he knocked.

"Come in, Bainbridge, I've been warned."

The warm voice rumbled out through the door. It was deep and jolly and put Vicky in mind of a pleasantly rotund gentleman with side whiskers. When she actually found herself face-to-face with Inspector Dougal, she discovered this interpretation was wholly incorrect. He was slender and clean shaven, younger than she had envisioned with a charming, if perhaps not handsome, face. He could certainly be dashing, Vicky concluded, in the right circumstances. His current situation saw him poised on the arm of a leather sofa at one end of his office, about to jump down onto a cheap looking pocket watch. He was bending his knees and swinging back his arms like a swimmer about to jump into a pool. Vicky watched him with alarmed fascination.

"Hello Bainbridge. Happen to know how much force it takes to break the glass on a pocket watch and cause it to stop?"

"I do not, I am afraid," Bainbridge confessed.

"Nor do I," Dougal admitted as he launched himself from the arm of the sofa and landed with great precision on the pocket watch. It failed to break.

"Curious," said the police inspector as he stepped off the unharmed timepiece. It was still ticking.

Victoria opened her mouth to say something but was not precisely sure what would be appropriate in the circumstances, so shut it again. Bainbridge walked across the carpet and examined the watch.

"Utterly unharmed," he said. "Not even a crack. In my experience, the glass only breaks when something small and hard pierces it, or if you were to throw the watch from a great height onto a pavement, for instance."

"You echo my own thoughts on the subject," Dougal rubbed his chin thoughtfully. "We've got a man dead in his own study, fell face down on carpet, most likely a heart attack. The only snag is his pocket watch, which we found under him with the face smashed. The simple assumption is when he fell his body weight smashed it, but having done a handful of experiments, I don't think that would be the case."

"Ah, so the watch is telling a different story to the body?" Bainbridge said.

"Precisely. I am not saying that changes things. Probably was a sudden death, but how did the watch smash? Loose ends bother me, Bainbridge."

"As they do me, which reminds me, this is my niece, Victoria Bovington."

Victoria wasn't sure what to say about the inference that she was a loose end. She opted to say nothing and smiled at Inspector Dougal as he gave her a polite bow.

"Charmed," he said, and his smile grew. "I never knew the Colonel had a niece. What are you doing here?"

"Just visiting," Bainbridge said before Victoria could speak. "Vicky happens to have a car and kindly drove me here."

Victoria again wanted to pull a face at him for making out she was not important. She restrained herself.

"It is pleasure to meet you, Inspector."

"You drive a car?" Dougal said with a mix of astonishment and admiration. "By Jove!"

"Nothing to it, really," Victoria shrugged.

"Ah, you ought to be offered a seat!" Dougal suddenly remembered himself. He rushed to the sofa and removed various papers, a long green scarf, and a pair of binoculars from its seat so his guests could sit down. Bainbridge was fully aware this was for Victoria's benefit, not his. Dougal never offered him a seat.

Dougal waved a hand at the sofa with that same strange grin on his face. Victoria carefully sat down, alert to the possibility of other forgotten items being upon the sofa cushions. Bainbridge sat down beside her.

"Now, this is about Mr Ward, is it not?" Dougal asked,

retrieving the watch from the floor, and shoving it in his pocket.

"It is," Bainbridge said, becoming serious. "I never thought I would see the day that Franklin would be arrested for murder."

"Nor did I," Dougal agreed. "Though, the lad has had his fair amount of run-ins with people. You know he is always getting into fights."

"I also know he always takes the worst of it," Bainbridge snorted. "The boy punches like an old woman. Actually, now I think about it, he punches worse than a lot of old women I know."

"I'm not denying it was accidental, in a sense," Dougal said. "He never meant to kill the fellow. It was a lucky blow."

"Franklin must have been falling forward from a great height to have any weight behind the punch," Bainbridge countered.

Dougal sighed.

"I do not like it, Bainbridge, I really do not. I have examined the thing from every angle, but the evidence is plain. Simon One-Foot took a blow to the stomach last night that resulted in a ruptured appendix. The doctors inform me it was probably about to burst, anyway. There would not have been much they could do for him, but the blow to his belly made things worse and he died in agony in the early hours."

"That is manslaughter, at the most," Bainbridge pointed out. "To suggest Franklin be tried for murder and lose his life over a brawl that was started by this Simon fellow is preposterous."

"That ought to be the case," Dougal agreed. "Except I have three witnesses claiming the fight was over and Simon had gone to shake Franklin's hand, when Franklin lashed out. That muddies the water. He was intending to hurt Simon when the man's guard was down."

"However, Inspector, Franklin tells a different story," Victoria piped up. She had been listening keenly and was beginning to feel alarmed and angry for Franklin, who was a victim here, rather than a killer. "Franklin says Simon knocked his lights out and he awoke sometime later in the gutter, quite alone."

"And my witnesses state that Franklin was not unconscious when Simon went to shake hands. He managed to punch Simon and then in an automatic response, Simon struck him on the head and sent him back into the gutter. Then he was unconscious," Dougal raised his hands in a sign of defeat. "I do not say I am happy about the whole thing, but I am conscious of the evidence I have before me and how it shall look to the judge and jury who try this case. Franklin's version of events is only backed by Franklin, while the other side of the story has three witnesses, all of whom were with Simon as he perished."

"They were also his cronies," Bainbridge snorted.

"More reason to believe them, then," Dougal replied. "They would not have harmed their friend and they would want his murderer caught."

"There has to have been someone else about," Victoria burst in, her ire mounting. "Someone unbiased who could say what really occurred."

"I have constables exploring that possibility," Dougal assured her. "I don't want to see an innocent man suffer any more than you do. However, I am bound by the facts before me, even if I am not convinced by the interpretation of them."

"I am informed Franklin was in a bad way when you arrested him?" Bainbridge changed the direction of the conversation. Victoria was getting rather stirred up, it would do no good to lash out at Dougal who was their ally in all things.

"He was," Dougal nodded. "I have had the police surgeon take a look at him. He says he is lucky to still be able to walk and talk, by the looks of things."

"Franklin, I think we can all agree, has a thick skull," Bainbridge said.

"That is true enough," Dougal smiled weakly. "I shall

make a point of indicating in my report that he was clearly suffering from various injuries and likely was not thinking straight at the time of the incident."

"You might also point out he was fighting for his life. Self-defence surely offsets this murder charge?" Victoria snapped hotly.

Dougal turned to her with a sad expression on his face.

"It comes down to timing," he explained. "Had Franklin landed the deadly punch during the struggle then manslaughter with the consideration of self-defence would certainly be a viable option. However, I have witnesses telling me the fight was over, that Simon was going to shake hands…"

"As if it was a fair fight!" Victoria snapped. "You ask me, that thug got what he deserved! Throwing his weight around and hurting someone who was doing him no harm!"

Inspector Dougal gave her a hurt look, taking her anger personally.

"The law is rather black and white about things," he said. "It is both its strength and its weakness."

"Then a poor man will hang for being beaten up in the street?"

"Victoria, calm down," Bainbridge told her fiercely. "We are far from finished as yet and the inspector is not our enemy. He has his hands tied by the strictures of the law, as things should be. The world would be a worse place if policemen could just do as they pleased. Fortunately, he also has us to root around in the dark corners he is not allowed to look in."

Dougal turned to Bainbridge and gave him a grateful smile.

"Accurate, as always, Colonel. I do not want to send Franklin before the magistrates with the way things are right now. My men are coming up empty-handed, since the people they need to speak to are not on good terms with the police."

"I understand," Bainbridge promised him. "I shall need the names of the men who claim to have witnessed

Franklin killing Simon One-Foot."

Dougal rose and went to his desk at the other side of the room, before returning with a paper. He handed it over. Upon it, neatly written out, was a list of three names.

"Who reported the crime?" Bainbridge asked.

"When it was obvious Simon was severely ill, a doctor was summoned. He noted the bruising upon Simon's stomach and inferred his death was not simply a result of an unfortunate medical situation. He reported the matter to the police."

"As I suspected," Bainbridge said. "The doctor's name?"

Dougal took out a fountain pen and scrawled a name at the base of the list.

"You are implying Simon's friends sold me a story to avoid implicating the real killer?" Dougal grinned. "I have considered that too."

"And what conclusion have you arrived at?" Bainbridge asked.

"That, such as the case is, the chances of me discovering the real killer are slim. You know what these sorts are like. They are more fearful of their neighbours than the police, and you can hardly blame them."

"Yet the truth must out, else an innocent man shall pay the price."

"Exactly."

Bainbridge rose from the sofa and Victoria followed suit. She still looked angry and when Dougal politely bowed to her again, she could not bring a smile to her face in response. Despite what her uncle had said, she felt the policeman was not doing enough to uphold justice. If a person could not rely on a policeman to discover the truth, then what hope was there?

It seemed to Victoria, as they left the office, that a veil had been lifted from her eyes and her youthful ideas of a benevolent legal system that always got the right fellow for the right crime were suddenly being dashed before her. She felt a touch ashamed by her naivety.

"You should not have been so hard on the inspector,"

Bainbridge informed her as they returned to the car.

"But he knows Franklin is innocent," Victoria protested.

"He does not know. He hopes," Bainbridge said. "Which is very much what I am doing. An instinct is not the sort of evidence you can use in court at a trial."

"Then, he would just let an innocent man swing?" Victoria returned, horrified.

"No, of course not. Dougal would figure something out, but he knows his limitations, which is why he is always willing to work with me. I fill the void between truth and lies which sometimes cannot be penetrated by the police."

Bainbridge hoisted himself up into the car, trying to fool himself into believing he was getting better at doing so. Victoria effortlessly hopped into the driver's seat and clasped both hands on the steering wheel.

"You make me feel as if I ought to apologise to the inspector."

"You should, at some point, but I am sure he shall survive your righteous outrage. Actually, I think it did him good to be reminded of the emotion behind all our discussions of law and justice. Your anger might spark something in him. Even Dougal sometimes gets a little despondent over things."

Bainbridge watched Victoria depress foot pedals and heft a brass lever backwards and the car started to steadily roll forward. If it wasn't for the fact Bainbridge sometimes suffered from pain in his hips and knees when he walked these days, he would have grown impatient with the snail pace of the machine. But he rather liked to rest his bones.

"What next?" Victoria asked him.

"We are going home, it is nearly lunchtime," Bainbridge answered, examining his watch to confirm the rumblings of his stomach.

Victoria looked disappointed.

"Are we not going to seek out this doctor and speak to him?"

"All in good time, first we shall have some nourishment inside us," Bainbridge paused. "We?"

"Well, you need the car," Victoria said defiantly. "And no great detective ever works alone."

"Hang on, are you suggesting…"

"I am merely being practical," Victoria said swiftly. "You need transport to wherever you must go, and I have a car. I would never forgive myself if I were to let you simply walk."

Bainbridge felt he was being ambushed. In fact, he was certain of it. He was going to have to put an end to this, at once.

Chapter Five

Mrs Huggins always served a sizeable dinner, knowing that the colonel was prone to skipping meals when working a case and needed to be 'fed up' to offset this deficit. It was, after all, the prerequisite of a good housekeeper to ensure her charge was well fed at all times. Bainbridge tucked into cold pressed tongue, homemade pork pie, cheese and crackers, and several rounds of freshly baked bread. This was all rounded off with iced tea, which was a habit Houston had brought with him from the States. It had taken years to convince Mrs Huggins to make it. She felt it was a slight on the English way of drinking tea.

Victoria cast her eyes over the small banquet Bainbridge was tucking into and helped herself to some cheese and crackers. Bainbridge cast a disapproving eye over the small quantity of food upon her plate.

"Are you not well?"

Victoria raised an eyebrow at him, curious at the question.

"You are not eating."

"I rarely have luncheon," Victoria explained.

"That's the trouble with girls these days, always fretting about their figures," Bainbridge snorted. "Regular meals are vital to a healthy body and mind."

"I shall take that into consideration," Victoria smiled.

Bainbridge was not satisfied but there was more to his irritation than just the poor amount of food on Victoria's plate.

"Look, I don't need looking after," he said abruptly.

Victoria glanced at him as she carefully halved a cracker with her knife.

"I never said you did."

"It is more what you imply," Bainbridge puttered. "I am not an invalid just yet, my girl. I am sure I have at least a few more years in me."

Victoria was silent a moment, thoughtfully cutting her cheese into small slithers. Bainbridge watched each cut as if it grated on his nerves. Why couldn't people just get on and eat things?

"Are you saying you do not want me around?" Victoria asked, just a hint of sadness in her tone.

Bainbridge backtracked fast.

"No, of course not."

"Do I disrupt your life terribly?"

"No, Vicky, no, you do not disrupt it at all."

"Am I of no value to you? Not one bit?"

"Now, that is ridiculous," Bainbridge blustered. "Of course you have value to me. I like your company, and you are my niece, after all."

"Does that mean you endure my presence for the sake of family relations?"

"Did I say that?" Bainbridge flapped one hand, dismissing her words. "When have I ever cared about family relations? No, I meant what I said. I have always enjoyed your company."

"Then why are you pushing me away?" Victoria said with that same sadness to her tone.

"I am not," Bainbridge spluttered. "Am I?"

"I am only trying to be kind and useful," Victoria said

tearfully. "I did not want you to feel I was merely using your hospitality. I wanted to be able to offer something in return. I thought, with my car…"

"The car is a marvellous idea," Bainbridge said firmly, completely failing to see the trap he had gladly walked into. "I very much appreciate the car."

"That is a relief," Victoria clutched a hand to her chest as if her heart might burst. "And you will continue to let me drive you around, so I might feel at least a little useful."

"I could hardly refuse," Bainbridge said, feeling graciously generous. "If it makes you feel better to take me about in the car."

"It does, it really does," Victoria assured him.

She suddenly straightened up and looked a lot brighter.

"Now that is settled, I am going to change my hat and I shall be ready with the car in, say, fifteen minutes?" Victoria glanced at a dainty ladies' watch on her wrist. "Then we shall be off to meet with the doctor who treated Mr One-Foot, I suppose."

She breezily walked out of the dining room, her crackers and cheese untouched. Bainbridge poked forlornly at his pork pie. He had a feeling he had been duped; he just wasn't sure how exactly.

He met Victoria at the car twenty minutes later, just for the principle of the thing. She did not comment but smiled at him happily. The engine was running, and the car was merrily vibrating, like a little bird flapping its wings in anticipation of the off. Still scratching his head over their conversation and what precisely he had let himself in for, Bainbridge made the undignified effort to climb up into the car and perch on the passenger seat. He was once again reminded of how much nicer it was to be driven somewhere than to have to walk. He could get used to this.

He even started to hum to himself as they trundled along.

"Why was he called One-Foot?" Victoria interrupted him, finding the humming like fingernails on a chalkboard and aiming for a distraction.

Bainbridge was briefly thrown by the question, then he remembered himself.

"I believe he earned the sobriquet due to having a club foot, thus he only has one good foot. Simon One-Good-Foot was a bit of a mouthful and so it was shortened. Street fighters always have nicknames."

He started to hum again.

"Did you know much about him?" Victoria interrupted once more.

"Mainly his reputation," Bainbridge answered. "Word of a man like Simon gets about. I do not believe he was ever in any serious trouble, however, outside of his illegal street fighting, of course."

"Just wondering who else might have wished him harm," Victoria said.

"Sorry?"

"Well, if Franklin did not deliver the fatal punch, someone else did. Stands to reason."

"Oh, yes, it does," Bainbridge felt flustered again, as if Victoria were two steps ahead of him all the time. Bainbridge was a good detective, but his brain worked at its own pace and sometimes took a while to bring together ideas. He didn't like that Victoria was suddenly telling him how to do his job.

"Turn down here," he said, trying to regain control of the situation. "The doctor's house is just there."

Dr Elliot lived above his surgery. He was one of those doctors who had fallen through the gaps in society and drifted somewhere in their own limbo. He saw patients from both the lower middle classes and from the distinctly working class. Not all his patients could pay him, but Dr Elliot was a charitable sort and tended to ignore this issue, though his wife was constantly nagging him about it, especially when the bills were due.

He was the logical choice when Simon's cronies had gone off to fetch a doctor who would be both sympathetic and not pushy about payment.

Bainbridge gingerly extracted himself from the car. By the time his feet were firmly on the cobbles, Victoria had hopped down to the pavement and was busily examining the brass plaque outside the doctor's surgery door. Bainbridge clobbered his knee on the metal foot stand that was supposed to be helping him to descend, and limped over to Victoria, somewhat aggrieved.

"You will be wishing to keep an eye on the car?" Bainbridge suggested as he drew near her.

"No," Victoria said innocently. "I have removed the starter handle and hidden it behind the seats. No one can start the car."

Bainbridge thought through his next statement. There was no easy way to say he wanted to conduct his investigation alone and it would be best if she stayed with the car.

"I really think..." he began, just as the door of the surgery was opened.

"I knocked while you were getting out of the car," Victoria said to him, before smiling politely at the person behind the door.

The figure was a young man, probably somewhere in his late twenties or early thirties. He had very neatly arranged dark hair and looked at them with an intense gaze, until he gave up the effort and put on his glasses.

"That's better. My wife does not like me wearing them. Says they make me look old," he grinned at them. "How may I help you?"

"Colonel Bainbridge," Bainbridge announced. "and this is my niece Victoria. I hoped to have a quiet word about the recently deceased Simon One-Foot."

"Oh," Dr Elliot became sombre. "That was rather unpleasant, I must say. I couldn't save him, though I tried. It is not really the sort of talk to be had before delicate company."

Bainbridge was about to take the opportunity of this

bone thrown his way when Victoria interjected.

"Thank goodness we are not delicate company," she said. "My uncle is in very good health, very robust. Nothing you shall say will shock him or cause harm to his constitution."

Dr Elliot opened his mouth to explain that was not what he meant, but Bainbridge thought it was best not to let him suffer too long.

"We are both prepared to hear what occurred to Mr One-Foot," he said.

Dr Elliot was thrown by this. Seeing as there was not much else he could do, he stepped back and welcomed them into his surgery. There was a narrow little waiting room, which was currently empty, and Elliot had his office just behind with a good view over the yard at the rear. Bainbridge noted that next door had been washing their laundry and had hung several large pairs of bloomers on their linen line, in full view of the poor doctor's windows.

"I do not know what you think I can offer you," Dr Elliot said. "I had the unenviable task of explaining to Mr One-Foot's friends that there was nothing I could do for him. They suggested the hospital, but I explained they would not be able to do anything either. The situation was too far gone, and I feared the jolting of the journey to the hospital would merely worsen things and increase the poor man's suffering."

"It was a burst appendix, then?" Bainbridge asked. Victoria had moved to one side and was quietly examining some books in a case against the far wall.

"From the location of the pain and the sudden onset, I believe so. However, I feared there may have also been a rupture to either the stomach or intestines, due to the powerful blow Mr One-Foot had taken to the stomach," Dr Elliot shrugged. "My suspicion would be he had been suffering pains on and off for a while but had disregarded them. They would have been the warning signs."

"He died very fast," Bainbridge observed. "I have heard of men lingering several days with a burst appendix."

"Yes, it was sudden, hence my suspicion that something else had occurred to speed up his death. I would guess that the internal damage was severe enough to result in bleeding inside. By the time I saw him, Mr One-Foot was extremely pale, barely conscious and his heart was beating weakly. I could tell it would not be long."

Victoria wandered back over from the bookcase.

"What did his friends say had happened?" she asked the doctor.

"They gabbled out a few things, even said he had been kicked by a horse," Dr Elliot snorted. "But I saw the cuts and bruises to his knuckles and knew he had been in a fight. I've seen the damage a blow to the stomach can do, especially if there is a pre-existing issue."

"You decided to report the matter to the police?" Bainbridge added.

Dr Elliot gave another shrug.

"It was my duty."

"I don't suppose there is anything you can recall as being odd or out-of-place?" Bainbridge asked. "Something that caught your attention?"

Dr Elliot frowned.

"No," he said. "I just saw a man who had been beaten and was going to die of his injuries. It made me angry, truth be told. The violence of this world is heart breaking. I told the police because it was my civic duty. I hope whoever did it is caught and hung!"

"Let us just hope it is the right person," Victoria said under her breath.

Dr Elliot glanced her way and she smiled at him charmingly.

"Thank you, Doctor," Bainbridge concluded the interview.

He exited the house with Victoria and returned to the car. There was the usual ordeal of climbing aboard, which was compensated for by the comfort of being seated.

"Where to next?" Victoria said as she started the vehicle.

Bainbridge stared thoughtfully at the bonnet of the car. "Well, Uncle?"

"Are you trying to become a detective, Vicky?"

"Heavens!" Victoria laughed. "What would give you that idea?"

"It is just…" Bainbridge felt the words melt away on his tongue.

"Why would I want to do something so ghastly as be a detective," Victoria continued, climbing into the car. "I mean, it is clearly work for men and men alone."

"You are being sarcastic now."

"Just a little," Victoria met his gaze. "Why does it concern you that I might find this whole matter curious? Are you afraid I shall get hurt if I follow you around?"

She had not added 'like Houston' but Bainbridge could fit that in himself easily enough.

"The detective business, it is not very respectable," he said.

"Nor is a woman driving a car," Victoria snorted. "I am not worried about respectable."

"It is dangerous, at times."

"I shall leave the dangerous bits to you, how does that sound?"

Bainbridge opened his mouth to bluster and caught her grin.

"Sarcasm, again."

"When shall you grasp, Uncle, that I am a very independent and determined person, and I do not want to simply be someone's wife. I want to do something worthwhile and feel I achieved something with my life."

Bainbridge wondered what he had achieved over the years and decided that was not a path he wanted to stumble down in that precise moment.

"I appreciate I have rather thrust myself into your life," Victoria continued. "And you are not used to a young lady in your house. No doubt we shall have challenges as we accustom ourselves to living with one another, but I see this as a truly good thing. I needed to get away from

44

Mother, and you should not be in that great house alone right now. We are assisting each other, Uncle."

"Julius," Bainbridge reminded her. "Uncle makes me feel old."

"Julius," Victoria responded. "We shall work well together."

Bainbridge let out a long sigh.

"I am going to regret this," he muttered to himself.

"Don't be silly," Victoria countered. "I shall be an asset to your investigative business. Now, what was the next address?"

"Your Mother will be furious with me," Bainbridge groaned.

"You seem to imply that would be unusual."

Bainbridge considered this.

"That is a fair statement. Well, if I must be damned, at least let it be in style," Bainbridge tapped the dash of the car. "Drive on Vicky and let us hope for the best."

Victoria grinned.

Chapter Six

"Here is our situation," Bainbridge declared as they paused outside a rundown house that by rights should not still be capable of remaining upright. There was a definite list to one of the walls, a gentle reminder that a fair few individuals in the building trade were rather slapdash in their attitude towards structural quality.

"Mr Stokes is unlikely to tell us anything beyond what he has already told the police and shall lie consistently. That will be the only thing consistent about him."

"Then why are we questioning him at all?" Victoria asked.

"Well, firstly because sometimes liars slip up," Bainbridge explained. "And secondly, because we need to rattle out a few more details concerning the events of last night. Stokes will lie about what he thinks he needs to, but he will be honest about other things that he deems unimportant and those will be our clues into the whole affair."

Victoria mused over this for a while.

"If you are sure."

"It is a principle of detective work that never fails. I learned it from Houston," Bainbridge felt that familiar pang of loss at the memory of his friend. Would he ever be able to say his name without this bleak hole opening within his chest?

"And he was a Pinkerton?"

"Oh yes," Colonel Bainbridge smiled with pride at this. "A first-class agent for the organisation. He joined in 1868 and one of his earliest jobs was protecting a state governor from being assassinated by gangsters in Chicago. I believe he was trying to put through some legislation that would make it harder for the thugs. Anyway, Houston was shot in the process."

"Oh dear!"

"It was only in his backside. Just a flesh wound. He loved telling that story at posh dinners," Bainbridge sighed to himself. "I used to get so tired of that tale and now I would give anything to hear him going on about it one last time."

"Why did he leave the Pinkertons?" Victoria asked, distracting him.

"I think he didn't like the direction the company was going in. He never really spoke about it."

They were being watched by a one-eyed cat perched precariously on a window frame that looked fit to fall to pieces at any moment. Victoria took a good look at the house before them.

"Does Mr Stokes own this whole place?"

Bainbridge tried not to sound condescending at her naivety.

"He rents a room."

"Just one room? Where does he sleep?"

"I imagine he does all his living within the said one room," Bainbridge explained. "Many people do."

Victoria frowned at the house. A whole new world was opening up before her.

"You shall learn," Bainbridge patted her hand, then he attempted to knock on the door.

The door had not been latched, or possibly the latch was as decayed as the rest of the property and incapable of holding the door. The thin wooden door wobbled inwards and slipped on its hinges so that it dropped down by an inch on the inside of the hallway.

"Why did you want to do that?" grumbled an old man who was in the doorway of the nearest room. He was sitting in rocking chair with a rug pulled over his knees.

"I has to lift it up to get it to fit right again."

The old man made no attempt to rise.

"How else were we supposed to indicate our arrival?" Victoria asked him.

"I don't know," the old man puttered. "Everyone who lives here knows to lift up the door and open it. No one knocks, except the debt collectors."

The old man gave them a sour look.

"Are you debt collectors?"

"Hardly," Victoria said as she stepped into the hallway.

"They usually send big intimidating blokes. Not two people who look like your grandfather and his nurse," the old man added.

"Mind your tongue," Bainbridge muttered.

"Exactly," Victoria backed him up. "This hat costs far more than a nurse could afford, especially on a salary my uncle could provide."

The old man gazed up at the aforementioned hat, doing some difficult mental arithmetic. Bainbridge contemplated what Victoria had just said and felt even more offended than before.

"So, you are her uncle?" the old man grinned lecherously. "Oh yes, I've seen many an 'uncle' escorting his 'niece' places. Though never here. Who could afford such as her, here?"

Victoria was finding this new train of conversation of a similarly confusing nature to that regarding Stokes only living in a single room. Bainbridge decided it was time he took the reins firmly and stopped this conversation.

"Where is Mr Stokes? I need to have a word."

"He can't afford her," the old man snorted.

"Hang on, I have just realised your implication!" Victoria said in horror. "You terrible old man! I am not a woman to be bought. I am a detective, and this really is my uncle."

It was the old man's turn to look baffled.

"That makes less sense than my theory."

"Not really," Bainbridge placed himself between Victoria and the old man. "We need to speak to Mr Stokes concerning the death of a man last night."

"Ho ho," the old man rocked back in his chair, as if trying to get away from Bainbridge. "We had the police here too. They were asking about a dead man. I told Stokes I don't need trouble here. I am working on being respectable."

"I fear you need to work a lot harder," Victoria interjected.

"If you just inform us where to find Stokes, we shall disturb you no more," Bainbridge said generously and knowing he was probably lying.

The old man glared at them both.

"He's got the room in the basement," he said. "Cheapest I have. There is a door under the stairs leads to it."

"Would it be too much to ask, to enquire if he is currently down there?" Bainbridge added.

"Well, he has not come up past me," the old man sneered. "And this house don't have a yard, or a back door. So, unless he went out a window…"

"Thank you," Bainbridge said and ushered Victoria away, though they did not go far as they were right on top of the stairs.

"That man is odious," Victoria whispered to Bainbridge. "Why were you so polite?"

"Because it pays in the long run," the colonel assured her.

"Is that one of Houston's tips?"

"No, that was a Bainbridge original," Bainbridge said proudly.

He had the door to the basement open and was looking down an exceptionally steep set of stairs. He tapped the ceiling over the staircase, which was barely above his head, to assess if it was likely to come down on them at any moment. He was not happy when his fist went through the plaster.

"What was that?" screeched the old man.

"Keep working on being respectable," Victoria responded. "You have a long way to go."

The old man was calling rude words at their backs as they headed down the stairs cautiously.

"You just destroyed the small trust I had developed between myself and that man," Bainbridge complained.

"You had developed nothing. The man is a toad."

"Vicky, tact is the key to great detective work!"

Victoria made a dismissive noise.

They reached another door at the bottom of the stairs and knocked.

"Mr Stokes?"

They waited.

"Do they usually answer?" Victoria asked.

"Mostly they do," Bainbridge nodded. "Not necessarily the guilty ones, but ordinary folks."

He knocked again.

"Possibly he has gone out, eluding our watchful friend upstairs."

"What was that?" Victoria said sharply.

Bainbridge froze, straining his ears.

"What?"

"I am sure it was a groan, as if someone were in terrible pain," Victoria said urgently. "Perhaps Mr Stokes has succumbed to the cruel violence of whoever killed his friend?"

Bainbridge was alarmed now. He turned the door handle and found it was unlocked, so he was able to let them both in. They hastened into a dark room, with a single narrow window casting light into it.

"Oi!"

50

Mr Stokes rose from the corner where he had been squatting. Bainbridge took in the chamber pot just as Victoria stifled a giggle.

"My apologies," Bainbridge said swiftly. "We thought someone was in trouble."

"You will be if you don't clear out and give a man some privacy!" Mr Stokes snapped.

"Yes, quite," Bainbridge was trying not to look in Stokes' direction and somehow kept failing. "We need to talk to you, but we shall wait outside."

He scuttled out with Victoria and shut the door. She leaned against the wall, shuddering with suppressed laughter.

"Damn you and your groans of a dying man!" Bainbridge hissed at her.

"I am amused you are more shocked than I," Victoria smiled. "We could assist Mr Stokes greatly by advising him about dietary fibre."

Bainbridge shook his head. He had burst in on some strange sights in his time, but a man on his chamber pot was a first.

They waited outside the door a long time. Victoria informed Bainbridge as each five minutes evaporated, using her wristwatch.

"You are dressed too smartly for these parts," Bainbridge winced as she informed him they had been stood there fifteen minutes. "Someone might think to rob you."

"They would be most unfortunate to contemplate such a thing," Victoria replied. "I went to a girls' school, do not forget, and we were taught a variety of self-defence specifically for young ladies. As our teachers said, this world is becoming increasingly dangerous and lascivious. A young lady must know how to protect herself."

"That is very good," Bainbridge conceded. "But I think you will find even your skills somewhat insufficient should a ruffian and his friends choose to come for your watch. Next time, don't wear it."

Bainbridge took another good look at his niece.

"And possibly a less expensive outfit too."

"I don't think I have a less expensive outfit," Victoria frowned.

"That is what I feared," Bainbridge sighed, then he knocked on the door again. "Mr Stokes, can we speak to you now?"

There was muffled swearing from the room and then Stokes paced across the floor and yanked open the door.

"Blow me! You are both still here!"

"It is important," Victoria informed him. "A man's life hangs perilously in the balance."

"Don't they all, love?" Mr Stokes gave her a lecherous smile.

He was a wiry man whose age might have been anything from thirty-five to sixty. He was the sort of person who had developed an agelessness that really meant they just could look old and young at the same time. He probably would look the same at eighty, if he lived that long. He had a smashed nose and broken front teeth, the hazards of being a street thug. He was shorter than Victoria and smelled of cheap tobacco smoke.

"We are here concerning the death of Mr One-Foot," Bainbridge interceded.

Stokes' attention snapped back to him.

"Nothing to do with me. I told the police who did it. I gave them a name."

"You did," Bainbridge replied. "But there have been further questions asked."

"Nothing to do with me," Stokes started to shut his door, but Bainbridge put his foot in the frame. Stokes went to slam the door shut and several shards of rotted wood broke off against Bainbridge's shoe.

"Look what you have done to me door!" Stokes bellyached.

"I suggest speaking to your landlord," Bainbridge said, trying not to think of the pain in his foot. "We shall not leave until you speak to us."

Stokes gave in grudgingly. He allowed him into his tiny corner of the world, which consisted of a narrow cellar, a bed in one corner, a stove and a hard chair in the other. Odds and ends of personal belongings reminded you the place had a tenant, such as the decaying rag rug on the floor and the cheap print stuck to the wall that declared 'All Sinners are Saved! Join the Salvation Army!' Bainbridge suspected it had been put there by a previous tenant. Stokes did not strike him as a man who was worrying about his immortal soul.

Stokes flopped back on his bed and pretended they did not exist. Victoria wrinkled her nose. The room had a scent to it that was cloying. It was a combination of damp, cooking, human body odours and general decay. It was unfortunate the window appeared not to open.

"You informed the police that Simon One-Foot was punched in the belly by Franklin Ward," Bainbridge said.

"No, I didn't," Stokes replied, surly.

"Then one of your cohorts did," Bainbridge corrected himself. "I want to know what happened last night."

"Simon picked a fight," Stokes shrugged. "The other guy punched him in the belly after they were done fighting. That was it for Simon."

"Why did he pick on Franklin?" Victoria asked.

"Why not?" Stokes growled back.

"At what time was the fight?" Bainbridge asked.

"How am I supposed to know that?" Stokes laughed humourlessly. "I don't have a fancy watch."

He had caught a glimpse of Victoria's wristwatch.

"Was it before midnight, or after," Bainbridge persisted.

"After," Stokes snapped.

"And where did it happen?"

"What is this?" Stokes said. "It was in Cattle Market Row."

"And Franklin threw just one punch to cause such injury to Mr One-Foot?"

"Yes!" Stokes yelled out.

"Surely a man like One-Foot was used to belly blows,"

Bainbridge added.

"Not like that, not out of the blue," Stokes shook his head. "That Franklin did for my mate and now he shall hang, and good riddance."

"One last thing," Bainbridge said calmly. "Did he punch him from the ground or standing up?"

"What?" Stokes asked.

"It is a simple enough question. Was Franklin still on the ground or was he stood up?"

"Simon was helping him up, alright? Now are you done?"

"I think so," Bainbridge winked at Victoria and started to walk away. She followed. He was almost out of the room when he turned around. "I'm curious, why was Mr One-Foot so nervous around Jimmy Black?"

"What?" Stokes said, but there was no longer just annoyance in his tone. He sounded worried.

"He ran away from Jimmy," Bainbridge said.

"He never ran! But Jimmy is mean, right? Really mean," Stokes had sat up. "But Simon never ran. He wouldn't. He was made of sterner stuff!"

"As you say," Bainbridge politely nodded his head towards him. "Good day."

Heading up the stairs again Victoria could not hide her disappointment.

"He told us nothing," she said.

"Did he?"

"Were you listening to a different conversation?" Victoria sighed.

"No and I think you are being too hasty. We now know the murder took place in Cattle Market Row. Do you know where that is?"

Victoria shook her head.

"No."

"Well, I'll tell you this. It is nowhere near The Toby Jug."

Chapter Seven

Before their next interview, Bainbridge guided Victoria to Cattle Market Row, a tight little street that once upon a time had been used to herd cows and other livestock down into the old market. Not only was the market no longer in use, but the road had been heavily built on and what had once been a reasonable-size walkway for herding large animals was now a small and pokey thoroughfare. It was also, as Bainbridge had stated, several miles away from The Toby Jug.

They parked the car at the top of the road and wandered down to assess the crime scene. There was not much to see.

"Did you note Franklin's extensive injuries?" Bainbridge asked his niece as he sauntered along almost carelessly.

"I did."

"That man bled a lot and blood leaves a mark," Bainbridge indicated the pale cobbles of the roadway.

"Maybe someone has cleaned it all up," Victoria said.

"You would be surprised how resistant blood can be to being washed off, especially when it has been allowed to dry a little. I shall not deny the possibility, however, I would not want to be accused of being close minded to the matter."

Victoria gave him a glare at his superior tone, knowing he was making a point about her earlier suggestion that he had decided Franklin was innocent before he had even spoken to him.

"This is not on the route from Flint's pub to The Toby Jug," Bainbridge observed. "Franklin has his flaws, but he is not the sort to traipse from pub to pub. No, I don't think Franklin was ever here."

Victoria had been glancing at the houses either side of them, mean, narrow properties that were cheap to rent but had nothing in the way of home comfort. She was wondering whether in places like this people might also spend their whole lives existing in a single room. She shuddered slightly at the thought.

"Are you here about the rats?"

An old woman had appeared at a door and was glaring at them. She was the sort of tiny, stout old woman who you didn't argue with because she was as stubborn as a mule and with the kind of strength you would never expect in such a tiny frame. She had wrapped her thinning hair beneath a head scarf and wore a pinny over her dress to protect her clothes as she worked. Her miniscule portion of the world was no doubt the cleanest spot anyone could ever find, and heaven help the person who walked mud in across her floors.

"Excuse me, Madam?" Bainbridge lifted his hat and addressed her as politely as he would a lady in a stately home.

"Rats," the old woman declared crossly. "I was told if I put in a complaint someone would come and look at them and tell me what was to be done."

"Oh yes," Bainbridge smiled. "Quite so, and where are the rats congregating?"

"What?"

"Where do you see them?"

The old woman gave him a suspicious glare as if to indicate she didn't trust people who used fancy words.

"Out in the yards," she told him. "I told them, in my letter, that my yard is clean as clean can be and the dustmen come regular."

"I see, then perhaps we should take a closer look," Bainbridge suggested.

Victoria gave him a nudge.

"What are you doing?" she hissed.

"Gathering information," Bainbridge grinned at her. "You will learn."

They followed the old lady into her small domain. It was, indeed, fastidiously tidy, the floors swept within an inch of their lives. The front door led straight into a sitting room with a fireplace and a staircase running up one wall. A door beside the stairs led to a passage to the back of the house. To the left was a kitchen with the shiniest pots and pans Bainbridge had seen in a long time. He almost winced as they sparkled light in his eyes. The old woman was hurrying to a door at the end of the passage which exited into her narrow yard. This consisted of bare, compacted earth, with a handful of paving slabs put down for good measure and to allow you to reach the privy at the bottom of the yard without walking on the dirt.

There were no obvious signs of rats.

"What an immaculate yard," Bainbridge declared. "I do not see such a thing often. My hat is off to you dear lady for your exceptional diligence."

Though she did not understand every word he had said, the old lady allowed herself to preen with pride at his obvious praise.

"I try," she said. "Not everyone does."

"And the rats?"

"Down by the privy," the old woman pulled a face. "I can't stand them. When you are sitting down to relieve a call of nature, they pop their heads under the door or worse."

The old woman shuddered, and Victoria had gone a pale

colour at the mere thought. Bainbridge was taking it all in his stride. Once, during a stint in India which had, somewhat to his relief, come to an abrupt end due to a mild case of malaria (Bainbridge did not like heat), he had found himself staring into the eyes of a tiger while using the barracks lavatories in the middle of the night. In contrast, rats held little fear.

"Very well, my assistant shall inspect the area for the purpose of our report," he said.

"I beg your pardon?" Victoria hissed at him.

Bainbridge gave her an amused smile.

"You did say you wanted to be a detective? This is part of the business."

"Looking for rats?" Victoria grimaced.

"In this instance, yes," Bainbridge replied then, in a louder voice, "Carry on my dear, make sure to check over the fences."

Victoria looked as if she would argue, then she swallowed her pride and walked purposefully towards the privy.

"She doesn't look the sort to be on a public hygiene committee," the old lady frowned, contemplating the letter she had sent off to that very same committee with her complaints. "I expected a man in overalls, or such."

"Oh, she is very philanthropic on the subject of public hygiene," Bainbridge said jovially.

"Does that mean she knows a lot about rats?"

"Near enough," the colonel propped himself against a wall and settled in for a short session of 'gathering information' in his somewhat haphazard but usually effective style. Houston had once said to him he considered Bainbridge rather like a giant sponge, absorbing lots of rather pointless information, but then squeezing out a few drops of important stuff. Bainbridge was not sure if he should be offended by that analogy or not.

"You know, we nearly did not come out today at all," Bainbridge said in a conversational tone to the old lady as Victoria opened the privy door and attempted not to shriek as a large brown rodent scuttled over her foot. "We heard there had been some trouble here last night and it was discussed whether it was prudent for us to come over today."

"Trouble?" the old lady frowned. "Are you referring to the fight out in the street? Things like that happen all the time."

"Yes, but generally the people involved do not kill each other," Bainbridge said, not looking directly at her, pretending he was just idly gossiping.

"Did you say someone died?"

"Yes, so I am told," Bainbridge agreed. "Fortunately, they have already arrested the man responsible."

"They have?" the old woman was listening keenly, Bainbridge thought he was onto a good thing with her, she seemed the type to watch out her windows and enjoy gossip.

"It is rather sad. How I was told the story a big street fighter chap picked a fight with a smaller fellow and beat him to a pulp, then as the big man went to help up his victim he was socked in the stomach and he died shortly after."

Bainbridge waited to see what response this drew. The woman wrinkled her forehead deeper and rubbed a finger along the edge of her chin.

"I don't know who told you that story," she said at last, "but it sounds nothing like the fight I witnessed last night. You sure it happened here?"

"Positive," Bainbridge nodded. "Why, what did you see?"

"Not a fight, not as you describe," the old woman explained. "More of an... an assault. I think that is the legal term for it when one fellow attacks another without warning."

"Ah, but that is what I described," Bainbridge said, sounding satisfied with himself. If he had judged her right, this would spur the old lady on to an in-depth explanation of how he was mistaken.

"That isn't it at all!" the old woman puttered at him. "You weren't listening. There was no fight, none at all. I was upstairs getting ready for bed – I rent this whole house you know, my husband left me well off," the old woman beamed with pride at this statement. "I was upstairs, and I can see easily down into the street from my window. I was pulling off my house shoes as I sat on the bed, facing the window and I heard these voices from below. Male voices. I glanced out as I like to know who is going past. I saw four fellows, one was very big and burly, taller than any man I know and looked meaner than one of them rats your assistant is looking for."

They both glanced in the direction of Victoria who had progressed in her investigation of the rat situation to standing on a wooden box to peer over the back wall of the yard. Bainbridge was satisfied she was doing a thorough job.

"Go on," he said to the old woman.

"These four men were walking in the middle of the road and I couldn't help thinking they looked like trouble and I was wondering if I had put the chain on my door. I do that at night seeing as I live alone and these days you can't trust anyone."

"Quite," Bainbridge nodded.

"I was watching them walk away when suddenly this other man comes running up behind them. The biggest man of the group, he was at the back, walking a few feet behind his friends who were laughing and joking. This new man comes rushing up behind him and shouts something, might have been his name. The big fellow turns around and the other man strikes him in the stomach."

"Gosh!" Bainbridge declared thoughtfully.

"As I said, no fight at all," the old woman was pleased with proving him wrong.

"What happened next?" Bainbridge asked.

"The second he had swung at the big man, the other chap starting to run off. Two of the fellows in the group began to chase him, while the third went to help his friend.

The big man looked in a bad way, anyone could see he took that blow hard. I even considered opening my door and having him brought into my house, but I didn't dare. You never know about people around here and what they might do to an old woman on her own."

"Naturally," Bainbridge nodded.

"The big chap, well he couldn't stand, and his friend couldn't hold him up. So he started yelling for the others to come back, which they did, and they gathered around the big fellow and helped him away. That was all I saw."

"It is quite different to the story I was told," Bainbridge agreed. "How peculiar."

"People are always talking rot and spreading rumours," the old lady snorted. "I don't know who it is the police have arrested, but if they think this happened in a fight, they were wrong."

"I don't suppose you could see much of the assailant?" Bainbridge asked.

"I never said anything about a sailor," the old woman glowered at him.

"No, I mean the man who attacked the big gentleman," Bainbridge explained.

"He didn't look anything like a sailor to me," the old woman had latched onto an idea and wasn't letting it go. Old ladies could be as dogged as terriers in this regard. "He was in ordinary clothes as best I could tell. We don't have streetlights down here, you realise."

"I was aware of that," Bainbridge assured her.

There was a cry from the bottom of the yard as the box Victoria had been standing on gave way and deposited her in a prickly bush.

"Oh dear," Bainbridge said, going over to assist her.

Victoria's hat was now askew, and she had been thrown into the bush in a way that made it difficult for her to right herself as her feet were flapping in the air. She was snagged in multiple places and even with great care there was the ominous sound of ripping as she was extracted.

Victoria scowled at her ruined dress as she stood before

them, then, with all the dignity she could muster, she spoke.

"Your rat problem is a consequence of your neighbours having a refuse pile against this wall," she told the old lady. "It is four feet tall, at least, and appears to be spreading."

"What?" the old lady scurried towards the wall, but even popping up on her tiptoes she could not see over it.

"What do I do?" she wailed.

"It is outside our remit," Victoria said firmly, glaring at Bainbridge. "I suggest you report them to their landlord or failing that, to the council as a public disorder issue."

The old woman was not happy about this and continued to protest as Bainbridge and Victoria left the house.

"But I thought you were with the public hygiene committee?" she cried.

"We have no power over unruly neighbours," Bainbridge explained. "If it had been an issue with the drains or something like that, well, then…"

"You mean you can't do anything?" the old woman said angrily.

Bainbridge propped his hat on his head.

"In that regard, madam, you are utterly correct," he assured her.

With that he departed the house, Victoria just behind him. He could feel her fury radiating off her like a fiery heat. He thought it best not to make eye contact as they returned to the car. Victoria clambered into the driver's seat and Bainbridge was about to climb up too when she put a hand out to stop him.

"Why did I have to look for rats?" she demanded.

"It was a distraction, so I could speak to the old lady and learn what she knew."

"How did you know she knew anything?" Victoria coughed.

"I didn't. I had a suspicion."

"So, I ruined my dress because of a suspicion?" Victoria threw up her hands.

"Yes," Bainbridge told her calmly. "Now, do you want

to know what I learned or not?"

Victoria sensed there was going to be no apology and as she wanted to be involved in this case, she grudgingly allowed him into the car and let go of her anger.

"Fine, but you owe me a dress."

"I did warn you about the detective business," Bainbridge said haughtily.

The look he received in response would have withered a weaker man.

Chapter Eight

"Plain as day it was a planned assault," Bainbridge concluded his retelling of the information he had gathered from the old woman. "The question we find ourselves with is why did Stokes and his friends feel it was necessary to lie about the situation."

Victoria was concentrating on negotiating the car around a group of children who seemed determined to keep hopping in front of her so they could get a better look at the vehicle.

"Will you get out of the way!" she honked her horn loudly at them. "I shall run you over, I shall!"

One of the little girls stuck her tongue out at her and danced in front of the car again. Bainbridge calmly reached out with his walking stick and dislodged an older boy who was clambering onto the back.

"Right, that is it!" Victoria declared and with a furious clanking and churning of gears she increased the car's speed. Veering around the farthest child, she sped forward and it was now apparent that it was too dangerous for anyone to dart in front of her and their spectators drifted off to some new sport.

Once they were around a corner, Victoria gently reduced the speed to a more sedate pace.

"I apologise for that," Victoria said to her uncle. "I quite lost my temper."

"I found the increased speed rather pleasant," Bainbridge assured her. "Why do we not go at that speed more often?"

Victoria looked uncomfortable and cleared her throat.

"You recall I said I received this car from Sven, my former fiancé?"

"Yes."

"I did not precisely mention when I received it. Which was yesterday, when he came to apologise about his dastardly behaviour and attempted to use this car as a means of buying me back."

Bainbridge thought about this.

"But you did not accept his apology?"

"Of course not! He has proven himself dishonourable and impossible to trust."

"Yet, you kept the car?"

Victoria gave him a sideways look.

"I was owed something for the humiliation, wasn't I?"

Bainbridge decided not to argue the point, considering he was quite enjoying using the car.

"Right-ho, if you turn down the next left, we should be close to the address of Mr White, who is another of Simon One-Foot's associates."

"About what you were saying earlier," Victoria said. "Why would Simon's friends not wish the police to locate the man who attacked him?"

"I can think of a few possibilities," Bainbridge said. "The one that seems most likely is that the person responsible for the assault is someone they are afraid of, so afraid of, in fact, they dare not tell the police the truth."

"But why drop Franklin in trouble, instead?"

"To distract the police and ensure they do not poke their noses into the matter. It was the doctor with the conscience that caused them bother. I have no doubt that Simon's friends would have done nothing about his death, certainly not have reported it, for fear of the person responsible. But that option was taken out of their hands and they had to, instead, think of a scapegoat."

"That makes sense," Victoria agreed. "Poor Franklin, he really has ended up in quite a pickle."

"Good thing he has us," Bainbridge smiled. "I believe the house we want is that one there."

There was a crumbling terrace house, of similar calibre to the one they had found Stokes in, set in the middle of a row. It looked as though it was being supported by its neighbours more than its own foundations. They stopped the car opposite.

"I suppose this is another of those places where people exist in a single room?" Victoria said with a cringe.

"You are learning," Bainbridge replied.

He lowered himself from the car, thinking how much walking he was saving himself, not to mention the fees for a carriage had he decided to hire one. How wondrous this invention of the car truly was. Houston would have loved it.

Yet again enthusiasm swung to grief and he had to shrug off the sensation as best he could.

Victoria was surveying the house, her nose wrinkling.

"Do you smell something?"

Bainbridge sniffed the air. He was not renowned for his sense of smell; it had been a failing Houston had often reprimanded him for. Apparently, a good nose was essential for a great detective. Bainbridge had a nose of considerable proportions and it might have been supposed it would grant him superior olfactory abilities. In contrast, it just seemed to mean he could sneeze well and snored loudly. He took a good whiff of the air, for appearance sake, and then shrugged at Victoria.

"Afraid I don't smell anything."

Victoria still looked concerned, but with no obvious sign of trouble she let the matter drop.

"Shall we knock?" she asked.

"I always do, begin politely, I say and hope for the best."

Victoria raised her hand and delicately knocked on the door. Several flakes of paint came away in the process. There was no response to her summons.

"I can definitely smell something," Victoria added, lifting her head, and sniffing the air.

"What sort of something?" Bainbridge asked, still nasally challenged.

"It is rather like smoke," Victoria said. "But not from a fireplace. Its rather like something is burning."

"Perhaps Mr White has set fire to his luncheon," Bainbridge reflected. "That would explain why he did not respond to our knock. He is trying to salvage it. Now you mention it, I do believe I am getting a whiff of fried liver and onions."

Victoria was ignoring him and peering through the window to their left. It was not the largest window, and someone had pasted newspaper across most of it, perhaps for privacy, or perhaps because the curtains hanging from the window were almost rags. Victoria bobbed down to try to peek through the grime.

"I do not think it is fried liver," she said, wrinkling her nose again. "It smells more like…"

She was interrupted by a flash of orange flame licking up the window and catching hold of the ragged curtains which went up in a whoosh.

"The house is on fire!" Victoria announced.

"That certainly would produce smoke," Bainbridge agreed, trying the door. It proved unlocked but was secured with a chain. "Damn!"

Bainbridge put his shoulder to the door and tried to force it.

"You better alert the neighbours Victoria. These houses are like tinder inside. The whole street will go up in flames if we are not careful."

Victoria obeyed, dashing to the house next door, and hammering on their front door until a woman appeared.

"What?"

"The house next door is on fire!" Victoria informed the woman.

Panic flickered on her face, then she disappeared inside and re-emerged with a baby and a toddler.

"That's Mr White's house!" she said as she escorted the children out into the road.

Victoria was already alerting others to the commotion, and they in turn were rousing their neighbours.

"Someone needs to find a policeman and have them send for the fire brigade!" Victoria called out randomly.

Bainbridge meanwhile was still trying to force the door. He was reluctant to thrust himself too hard at it, as he was not sure if he fell through whether he could easily get up again. The chain, unfortunately, was proving stronger than it appeared. Two men joined him at the door.

"Stand back," one told him, and he had barely moved away when they were slamming into the door and forcing it open.

"Oh, what if my house goes up?" wailed the woman Victoria had first alerted. "Where shall I live?"

Elsewhere in the road, a water chain was being arranged with buckets and pans being scavenged from the nearby houses. There was no running water in this road, but there was a pump in a little fenced area at the end, where everyone fetched water from. The water chain was stretching all the way to this pump and frantic efforts were being made to get enough water to douse the flames.

The two men who had battered down the house door had stumbled inside, coughing at the smoke which was now black and thick.

"Sammy?" one called, almost immediately choking on the smoke.

"He might be in the front room," Bainbridge called from the doorway.

He didn't add, if that was the case, he was more than likely already done for. The men stumbled on and he could hear them in the darkness, trying to locate the unfortunate

Mr White.

Victoria had walked the length of the road to summon assistance and was now returning.

"Has anyone gone for the fire brigade?" she demanded to the world at large.

The woman she had first alerted was weeping and rocking the baby in her arms and stared at her with pure misery on her face.

"My house, my house. Albert works so hard so we can have a decent home and now this."

Victoria patted her arm, though she knew it was little consolation and if the fire brigade did not arrive soon then the whole row might be doomed. She was just debating getting her car and driving off to find help when a small boy came racing into the street like he was personally on fire.

"Fire engine is coming!" he yelled at the top of his lungs.

"Thank goodness," Victoria sighed, then louder. "Right, everyone who is not doing anything needs to move to the far side of the road so the engine can get through."

She ushered the fraught woman up onto the pavement and handed her over to a couple of friends who did their best to calm her.

At the house, a handful of buckets of water had made it down the line and had been flung through the doorway, which as Bainbridge had pointed out to the man doing the throwing, was of very little use at all.

"The fire is in the front room, not the hallway!"

"How am I to reach that?" the man protested. "I can only see through this here door."

"I think going inside is the obvious solution."

"I'm not going in there! It's on fire!"

Bainbridge managed not to swear in frustration. Behind him, coughing and gagging, the two valiant men who had risked their lives looking for Mr White were emerging. Slung between them was the unfortunate householder who looked more dead than alive.

"Bring him over here," Bainbridge directed. "Lay him

on the pavement. And someone actually go into that house and throw water on the fire!"

This last he bellowed to the water chain.

"It was a mess in there," one of his helpers coughed. "Gin bottles on the floor and everything ablaze."

Bainbridge was checking for signs that Mr White was breathing. It was subtle, but he could just feel warm air on the back of his hand when he held it by the man's mouth. He checked his pulse and was relieved it seemed quite strong. In the distance, a bell was ringing, but he did not register it in his concern for Mr White.

"What do we do?" the other helper asked him, coughing into his sleeve.

"We give him plenty of room and see if he comes around," Bainbridge said. He was stripping off his coat to bundle up under the man's head.

At the top of the road the fire engine arrived and with its clanging bell it rumbled down the cobbles. It consisted of a carriage drawn by two horses, the fireman sitting upon it. Mounted on the carriage was a steam-powered water pump, a tank of water and a long hose. Behind the first carriage, another was swiftly following, the firemen in dark uniforms and shiny brass helmets.

"Clear the way! Clear the way!"

The water chain dispersed as the engines rolled forward and the firemen jumped down. The hoses were unfurled and as the horses calmly stood by, the steam powered pumps went to work and forced water through the hose. Bainbridge watched on with curiosity as the whole procedure occurred.

"Marvellous," he mumbled to himself.

"Julius!"

Victoria had arrived at his side.

"Are you hurt?"

"I am perfectly well," Bainbridge assured her. "I fear Mr White may need a doctor, however."

"He can't afford a doctor," one of the helpers said.

They all fell silent as they looked at the man on the

pavement. He had not stirred.

"Good job you came along," the other helpful man informed Bainbridge. "Whole road could have gone up."

"It still might," his friend said grimly.

The swoosh of water pushing through the hose was a relief to hear. Several firemen had to grasp onto it as it battled the surge. They looked as though they were wrestling a giant snake. Luckily, the fire had not spread as far as it might have and was still largely confined to the downstairs of the house. Black smoke was pouring out of the front window, which a fireman had smashed with a metal fire hook to make it easier to get water inside. The brickwork was stained with soot and it looked to Bainbridge as if it would prove necessary to demolish the house once the fire was stalled.

"A terrible thing to occur," he sighed. "Poor Mr White."

His helpers slowly drifted away, back to their work or to their own homes. Victoria and Bainbridge remained with Mr White, isolated to one side of the burning house, as the flames were slowly being tamed by the firemen.

"Do you think he will live?" Victoria asked her uncle.

"I would not like to say," Bainbridge replied. "His pulse is sound enough. I believe that offers hope."

Water was now pouring out of the front door of Mr White's home and one of the steam pumps had been stopped as the fire died. The second fire engine continued for a while longer, making sure there was nothing left to catch alight and some of the firemen were walking around the house to check for any secondary fires. It seemed the worst was over.

"Look at it," Victoria sighed. "What a mess."

"Poor Mr White," Bainbridge repeated.

Maybe he heard his name, or maybe it was coincidence, but Mr White gave a small groan and moved a little.

"That is a good sign?" Victoria asked her uncle.

He was not prepared to say too much, not yet.

"It is better than nothing," he answered, then he turned to the man on the pavement. "Mr White, can you hear me?"

Mr White emitted another groan, then his eyes flickered open.

Chapter Nine

Mr White was assisted into one of his neighbours' homes. He could not walk, and it required three burly men to carry him inside and lay him out on a sofa. The sofa was too small for him, so his feet stuck over one arm. Bainbridge remained outside, though Victoria was twitching to follow the poor man and discover how he was.

"Are we not going to speak to him?" she asked her uncle.

"All in good time," Bainbridge assured her. "First, I wish to speak to the firemen."

"Whatever for?" Victoria said, exasperated.

Bainbridge gave her a curious look then shook his head. "You have a lot to learn, my dear."

He wandered over to a fireman who was carefully winding the hose back around its wheel on the engine.

"Good day," Bainbridge said to get his attention.

The man glanced at him, his soot-covered face registering annoyance at being disturbed.

"I wish to speak with someone concerning the cause of the fire," Bainbridge persisted, blatantly ignoring the look.

Bainbridge heavily relied on being an irritating nuisance to get information. It was remarkable how often people would tell him things they otherwise would not say simply to get rid of him.

"You want Captain Shaw," the man said, and nodded roughly in the direction of a man who was assessing the structural damage caused by the fire to neighbouring houses.

"Thank you," Bainbridge said cheerfully, then he strolled over to Captain Shaw.

"Captain Shaw?"

The man spun around.

"What?" he said loudly.

"I asked if you were Captain Shaw?" Bainbridge repeated.

The fireman removed his brass helmet and waggled a finger in one ear.

"Completely deaf on my left side," he informed Bainbridge in a shout, though he probably considered it a perfectly normal tone of voice.

Bainbridge had approached from the man's left, so this seemed to explain his difficulty in hearing him.

"Very sorry to hear that," Bainbridge said.

"What?"

"Very sorry to hear that," Bainbridge said louder and with firm enunciation.

"No need to shout," Shaw snapped. "I'm completely deaf in my left ear."

"More like both ears," Bainbridge puttered to himself.

"What?"

"I was wondering if you had determined the cause of the fire?" Bainbridge said loudly.

"Can't discuss that with just anyone," Shaw said firmly and went back to tapping at a wall with a hammer.

Bainbridge was not deterred. He tapped Shaw on the shoulder.

"What?" the fireman spun around on him.

"You can discuss the cause of a fire with the insurance

company covering a property, can you not?"

Shaw frowned.

"Certainly."

"Good, that means you can discuss the matter with me."

The frown deepened.

"What?"

"I am from the insurance company who covers Mr White's home," Bainbridge persisted.

"People don't need fire insurance these days," Shaw said. "We are employed by the local authorities to attend fires anywhere."

"I appreciate that. My insurance firm is a charitable organisation that provides cover for poorer neighbourhoods in case of emergency, such as fire. We provide household insurance and those in our scheme have the security of knowing that should trouble befall them they have us at their backs."

"What..."

"Please, Captain Shaw, I can hardly speak louder."

"I was going to say, what are you doing here?" Shaw sounded suspicious.

"That, my good sir, is easily answered," Bainbridge said with bravado, which he was good at. "Mr White, the gentleman whose house has just burned down, was one of our customers. He recently stopped paying his premium and I had popped along to discover the cause and whether he wished to continue his policy. I arrived in time to discover the fire."

Bainbridge said this with aplomb, and it sounded a very good speech, but Captain Shaw looked unconvinced. Fortunately, at that moment Victoria appeared.

"I really think we should speak to Mr White," she said to her uncle.

"All in good time," Bainbridge said, trying to shuffle her away.

"You work in insurance too?" Captain Shaw asked Victoria.

Bainbridge bit his tongue, there was nothing he could

do now. Victoria glanced up at Shaw in surprise and there was an awful moment when it appeared she was going to cry ignorance and then suddenly the penny dropped for her.

"Why should I not be in insurance?" she asked Shaw.

This threw the fireman long enough for Bainbridge to take charge again.

"I really must know the cause of this fire and whether my employer is going to be required to pay out on Mr White's insurance policy," Bainbridge said. "Mr White was covered up until tomorrow, you know. You can understand my suspicion over the matter. A fire on the very last day the man was covered by insurance."

"It pays to be suspicious in insurance," Victoria added helpfully.

Captain Shaw looked most baffled by them both.

"Well," he hesitated. "I suppose, as you are in insurance, I ought to be helpful."

"It is really only a question of whether the fire was, in your opinion, started deliberately or accidentally."

Captain Shaw did not look entirely happy about the situation, but after he had considered things for a few moments, he concluded there was no harm in speaking about what he had seen.

"I should say it was a case of carelessness," he said at last. "Mr White was surrounded by a considerable number of bottles of beer and gin. The fire appears to have begun on the rug near the fire, and I should say the alcohol about the place assisted it. There were several bottles near the starting point of the fire, one or more could have spilled onto the floor. In the business of firefighting, we call that an accelerant."

Captain Shaw said this pompously, as if he expected them not to know about such things.

"Go on," Bainbridge said, not rising to his bait.

Shaw deflated a little.

"The actual cause of the fire was likely the pipe Mr White smoked. We discovered it charred on the rug. We didn't at first realise what it was, but one of my boys noticed its distinctive bowl shape and worked out its significance."

"Then, your theory is that Mr White having drunk himself into a stupor dropped his lit pipe. The ashes fell onto a patch of rug that was already saturated with alcohol and were hot enough to begin the fire," Bainbridge concluded.

"Precisely," Shaw nodded. "The fire then spread quickly across the alcohol-soaked rug, jumped up at the newspaper on the windows and raced along those ragged curtains. The whole room was a tinderbox. I cannot fathom why you would insure such a place."

"For peace of mind," Bainbridge said staunchly. "But as it appears this fire was a result of carelessness we shall probably not pay out."

Shaw still looked like something was niggling him about the whole situation and Bainbridge decided it was a good time to leave.

"Thank you," he said, lifting his hat once more.

"Don't suppose you cover the houses either side of Mr White's too?" Shaw asked.

Bainbridge froze, rapidly considering his options.

"Afraid not," he said, deciding it was better to err on the side of caution in case Shaw started doing his own detective work.

"Pity," Shaw tapped a wall again. "Looks to me like they are going to need it."

Bainbridge gave him a smile, then headed back into the road, Victoria hard on his heels.

"Well, what did that tell you?" she asked.

"Quite a lot," Bainbridge replied. "But before I speak, how about you say what it told you?"

Victoria crossed her arms and looked irritated by the question. It was a bit like the spot tests the teachers at her school sometimes did right at the end of a lesson, just when you thought you had got away without learning anything.

"It tells me that Mr White was a hopeless drunk," she

declared.

"A fair point," Bainbridge agreed. "However, we cannot conclude that from one conversation, not without corroborating evidence. Mr White's rescuers, for instance, seemed not to have been expecting lots of bottles in the front room. They made no reference to White being a known drunk. It could be they simply did not consider such a statement important, on the other hand, it could mean Mr White was not known for his drunkenness."

Victoria was confused by this.

"What does that mean?"

"It means that perhaps Mr White had drunk himself into oblivion not because it was his habit, but because something was gnawing at his conscience and he could only find peace within drink-induced delirium."

The confused look lifted from Victoria's face.

"I think I see what you are saying. He might have been drinking to forget what had happened to Simon One-Foot and how he and his friends had stitched up an innocent man."

"Very good," Bainbridge smiled. "Where on earth did you learn the phrase stitched up?"

"I read a lot," Victoria grinned at him. "I have read everything about your cases. All the bits in the newspapers. Mother detests newspapers in the house."

"Your mother always was adamant that ignorance was bliss," Bainbridge sighed. "Now is the time to speak to Mr White, would you agree?"

"I do, but was it really so important to speak to the fireman?"

"Never ignore information, Vicky. You never can be sure when it will be important."

Bainbridge led the way into the house where Mr White had been taken. The poor man was lying still, propped on the sofa, barely conscious. Two women were tending to him, washing his face and hands, and trying to get him to take a sip or two of tea. They gave Bainbridge and Victoria rather fierce glares as they stood in the doorway.

"We apologise for the intrusion," Bainbridge said at once, removing his hat and endeavouring to look as meek as possible. "We hoped to see how Mr White was doing."

"Were you the ones who raised the alarm?" the younger of the two women asked.

"Yes, dear lady, that would be us," Bainbridge answered.

The two women exchanged glances. There was a moment of silent understanding between them, then they returned their gazes to the intruders.

"You best come in then," the younger said. "Mr White is in a bad way."

Bainbridge and Victoria shuffled into the room.

"How bad?" Bainbridge asked.

The younger woman shrugged.

"Captain Shaw, one of the firemen, informs me he believes the fire was begun by Mr White's pipe falling onto the rug," Bainbridge elaborated.

"Ah, that could be right," the older woman sighed. "Right hooked on that pipe he was, never did anything but smoke it."

"Did Mr White drink?" Victoria asked abruptly.

Bainbridge gave her a look. The question was too blunt, too brusque.

The women seemed thrown by it too. The older one finally spoke.

"That's quite a question."

"They found a lot of bottles in his front room," Bainbridge explained. "The firemen are suggesting Mr White became very drunk and dropped his lit pipe near a spillage of alcohol."

The older woman glared at him.

"Never heard of such a thing in all my days," she snorted. "Mr White was a decent fellow, even if he did hang around with that awful giant. I told him hanging around with that sort would be his death."

"Do you mean Simon One-Foot?" Victoria asked.

Bainbridge wanted to give her a nudge for being so

obvious. The first trick to questioning someone was not to reveal how much you knew.

"You've heard of him?" the older woman was looking very suspicious now.

Bainbridge decided the only option was to come clean and hope the ladies were understanding.

"We do know of Mr One-Foot. A friend of ours has been accused of causing his death by accident. Naturally, our friend denies this, claims, indeed, that he was a victim of that thug. Unfortunately, the police are not listening. We had hoped to speak to Mr White and learn what really happened last night."

"Simon is dead?" the younger woman repeated to herself. "Well, well."

"Never liked him," the older woman said firmly.

Bainbridge was beginning to think they were mother and daughter, there was a similarity in their mannerisms and speech that was telling.

"I don't think you will be getting much out of Mr White any time soon," the older woman added. "But I will say this. He was not a drinker. He lived alone and worked hard at the shoe factory. Aside from his association with that Simon One-Foot, I considered him a man of sound judgement."

"You talk as if he is already late for this world," Victoria said uneasily.

The old woman did not flinch.

"That may very well be the case," she replied, there was no hesitation in her voice. "Time will tell."

"Thank you for your assistance," Bainbridge said, pulling a thin slip of card from his pocket. "Should Mr White recover, might one of you ladies inform me? Equally, if the worst should occur, I would like to pay my respects."

The older woman took the card and gave him a nod of her head to indicate she would do that.

"Thank you again," Bainbridge donned his hat as he left the small house.

"Things do not seem to be going well," Victoria reflected as they headed for the car.

"Nonsense, we have barely begun," Bainbridge brushed off the comment. "We have learned something very useful."

"Have we?" Victoria raised an eyebrow at him.

"Yes, we have learned that Mr White was feeling quite troubled by recent events. If he recovers, that gives me hope he will be willing to talk about things."

"And if he doesn't recover?" Victoria asked.

"I prefer to focus on positive outcomes," Bainbridge said firmly, hauling himself up into the car. He had yet to discover a way to do this gracefully.

"Where to now?" Victoria asked, alighting with elegance.

Bainbridge endeavoured not to be envious of her grace, considering she was his niece and all, but he felt like a waddling hippopotamus alongside her, which was not the sort of imagery conducive to a man's self-esteem.

"Julius?"

"Hm, what?"

"I said where to now?"

"Oh," Bainbridge came back to reality. "Home, I think. Yes, home."

"But it is only late afternoon," Victoria bewailed.

"Nearly dinnertime then," Bainbridge said with glee. "Besides, I smell like a smoked kipper and must change at once."

Victoria did not look pleased.

"Should we not talk to the last of One-Foot's associates, at least?"

"No," Bainbridge said calmly. "I would rather he has time to hear about Mr White's accident and to consider its implications before we go see him. I think that might be very prudent."

Victoria sighed and put the car into gear, turning it around in the street with great care and a lot of going back and forth.

"It was a good thing we came to see Mr White," she

observed as they finally pointed in the right direction.

"I imagine that depends on your perspective," Bainbridge said darkly.

Chapter Ten

Bainbridge retreated to his study as soon as they returned home, stating to Victoria that he required some space to think. This was not untrue, but while she might have supposed he was considering the case, in reality, he was thinking about his late partner, Houston, and his sudden demise.

Bainbridge found he went through these periods with his grief. At points he could be almost oblivious to the pain that burned inside, the utter fury that Houston had been snatched unceremoniously from this world. That had been how he had felt during the day as he travelled around with Victoria. Then would come the flipside, the utter and intense despair that felt as if it would engulf him and eat him whole.

Not to mention the terrifying loneliness that infected his heart. He had never imagined he would be without Houston. He had been older, after all. He had had a few health niggles over the years that had made him question his longevity. They had always joked about how Houston would outlive him and could inherit his estate, since there was no one much else who he could leave everything to. Houston had always seemed so very alive, whereas Bainbridge...

Bainbridge just felt old and sore. He felt tired and wondered how much longer he had to endure this heartless world where good people were snatched away without a thought. He was not religious and did not think there was an afterlife where he might collide once more with Houston. No, his friend was lost to him for good and the pain of that was unbearable each and every time he remembered.

It had been on the car journey home that Bainbridge had been struck by his grief, rather like a blow to the chest. He could not say what had triggered the sudden emotion, it had just overcome him and left him feeling as if he might not be able to breathe anymore, as if he might just fall out of the car and die himself. A part of him wanted to, another part was terrified by the thought.

Bainbridge had been raised not to show emotion, to encase it within himself and build stout walls around his feelings. Houston had teased him over that, but Americans were always over emotional and that was not something to be gleeful about, as far as Bainbridge was concerned. However, this keeping everything inside was not as easy as letting everything loose and he was struggling to keep up his calm façade by the time they pulled up to the house. Hence him making his excuses and retreating to his study where he could be alone to express whatever it was that needed to be expressed.

Only, the moment he sat at his desk, the moment he was free to cry or shout, or anything, in that moment his emotions dried up and nothing came out. He stared at the top of his desk, at the papers and pens, the unfinished correspondence, and there was a hollow nothingness inside him that was somehow even worse.

Houston had made the world a better place for Bainbridge, had stilled the nagging doubts that infested the colonel's heart. Without him, the world was bitter, barren, and empty.

"Why were you at that bank?" Bainbridge said to himself.

It was the same question he asked himself every time Houston sprang to mind, and he never had an answer. He had come to the conclusion that Houston had been investigating something without him, but what might that have been and why had he kept it a secret from Bainbridge?

"You were a damn fool," Bainbridge scolded his dead partner. "You should have told me."

The grief had reached its deepest and was now receding once again. It was like running up and down hills, the grim climb to the top where things were near enough normal, and then the treacherous slide down again to the bottom where things were at their worst. Bainbridge was on the climb up again, which was a relief, though it was only a matter of time before he reached the summit, and he would slip once more.

Still, you could not worry about the future. That had been one of Houston's mottos.

"Perhaps if you had worried about it you would still be with us," Bainbridge sighed to himself, then he started sifting through his correspondence.

There were a lot of condolence letters, many from people whose names he did not recognise. Was one supposed to respond to them all? He really did not care to. Thinking of the hours it would take to write adequate replies and ready them for the post made him feel exhausted before he had begun. He put them all to one side and instead turned to the newspaper he had left on the desk the day before. Bainbridge had a passion for newspapers, they were a wondrous source of information on human nature and brought him endless fascination. He endeavoured to read all the local papers and a number of nationals on a weekly basis. Sundays had always proved a good time for them.

The paper on his desk was the Eastern Daily Press, one of the local papers. He had been halfway through it when he had slipped out for his visit to the prison.

He now retrieved it and returned to the page where he had left off. A lot of the page space was devoted to gardening and household tips, adverts for cure-alls and wanted advertisements – WANTED – reliable boy for work as footman. WANTED – position for a housemaid, full references provided. WANTED – piglets to bring on. Will pay reasonable price.

Bainbridge trawled through the adverts, noting all the many complications of peoples' lives, the men and women desperate for work or to find good employees. The farmers needing or selling stock. The bachelors looking for a wife, the spinsters looking for husbands. Everyone wanted something, or so it seemed.

He turned the page and scanned through several more rows of adverts before returning to some articles of actual news. There were concerns about the price of wheat, fears of a shortage of animal feed through the winter, weather reports on more warm weather to come and then, just as he was growing tired of the dross of it all, he saw something that caught his eye and made him pause.

On Saturday night, a boxing match will be held at the Corn Exchange, the participants being Duncan Head, English boxing champion and newcomer Simon Underwood, who is hoping to begin his legitimate fighting career. Tickets are available, but please may we remind readers that betting on the outcome of this encounter is frowned upon and anyone found doing so shall be reported to the officials.

Bainbridge paused. Could it be? Simon One-Foot had to have a more conventional surname and he might have grown tired of street fighting and considered taking a more respectable route. The question was, if Simon Underwood and Simon One-Foot were one and the same, did this proposed match have any bearing on the man's death? Bainbridge considered the article a while longer, then decided he wanted a second opinion. He left his study and wandered about the house until he found Victoria in the front room. She was attempting to repair her torn dress.

"That is not very good," Bainbridge observed.

Victoria glowered at him.

"Mrs Huggins does not darn or sew apparently, thus I am limited as to my options."

"I am sure we can find you a seamstress."

"It is a matter of cost," Victoria sniffed. "I am currently rather out of funds."

"Ah," Bainbridge said. "Well, then…"

"Do not suggest it," Victoria raised a hand to warn him. "I must endure. I shall not be forced back to Mother because of a shortage of money."

"Did you not bring any with you?" Bainbridge asked.

"I confess, I somewhat overlooked the matter," Victoria admitted. "I have not really had need for it before."

"Running away is a tad more complicated than you surmised," Bainbridge guessed.

"I have made some errors, but I shall find a way to adjust," Victoria asserted. "I was considering, for instance…"

"No," Bainbridge said firmly.

"You have not heard me out."

"And yet I can guess you are about to suggest you become my partner in the detective business," Bainbridge replied.

"The thought had crossed my mind," Victoria said sullenly. "That way I could earn my own income and be free of my family ties."

Bainbridge shook his head.

"The detective business is difficult and dangerous."

"We have had this discussion."

"Then we shall have it again. It is not a respectable career for a lady. It is barely respectable for a gentleman. I cannot encourage you in this matter," Bainbridge felt better with himself for being firm, then he remembered why he had come to find her. "Anyway, what do you make of this?"

He handed the newspaper to Victoria.

"I don't believe I require Squire's Invigorating Liver Pills," Victoria declared stonily.

"Not that, read this bit," Bainbridge pointed and with bad grace Victoria read.

"Well?"

"Well, what?" Victoria asked.

"What do you make of it?"

Victoria folded her arms over her chest.

"I thought you said I was not to become a detective."

Bainbridge's look of satisfaction fled as he realised what he had said and done. Fleeting emotions crossed his face.

"This isn't detective work," he said.

"Isn't it?"

"No, it is solving a puzzle for a friend."

"How odd that it has quite the appearance of being detective work," Victoria said sourly.

She had a look on her face that reminded Bainbridge all too well of her mother. He felt his resolve slipping.

"It is a nasty business, being a detective," he countered, feeling that sense of failure already.

Victoria just stared at him sternly. Sometimes you could not win.

"You ought to know it is a very poorly paid profession, despite what some successful authors might have you believe when they invent detectives in novels," he added defiantly. "I am quite sure you will tire of it swiftly."

"When I do, I shall tell you," Victoria told him primly. "In the meantime, we are a team?"

Bainbridge tried to find another reason, other than the ones he had already used and failed with, to convince her not to become a detective. His mind was a terrible blank. When you had used the danger card without it having effect, what was left?

"Your mother would kill me if any harm befell you," he said at last.

"That would rather resolve your problem for you, would it not? Besides, what harm has befallen you all these years?"

Bainbridge opened his mouth, thinking of many encounters with men with knives and guns that had ended with near misses, though he never had actually been injured during one. There was, however, one thing.

"Houston," he said, and there was no need to elaborate.

Victoria paused, some of her fight slipping as he reminded her of his dead partner.

"He was on a case when he died?" she asked at last. "That was not what the papers said."

"No. I mean, I don't know. I have surmised," Bainbridge sighed. "I don't know at all, Vicky. I do not feel like I know anything, but it is my duty as your uncle to try to persuade you to reconsider. I do not want anything to happen to you."

Bainbridge's voice had trembled on that statement. His emotions were not so well contained as he had thought. Victoria smiled at him.

"The world is a dangerous place," she agreed. "But you cannot keep me hidden away from it. I shall not allow it. I must take my chances or else I shall die of sheer boredom and misery. I speak slightly flippantly, I suppose, seeing as I do not know that much about the detective business, but I do know I cannot continue my life as it is. I feel such despair at the mere thought, can you not understand that?"

Her sincerity touched Bainbridge and he smiled.

"I understand it all too well," he replied.

Victoria sighed.

"I appreciate I have rather jumped upon you, trespassed into your home, stepped on your toes. My reasons are simple enough. I was desperate," Victoria met his eyes. "I did not want to marry Sven. I saw my future with him, one of being a dutiful, dull wife with nothing in her life except endlessly mindless social engagements for my husband's benefit and a ridiculous number of offspring to ensure the continuation of his family name. I would be another of those women lost to history as just someone's wife. The notion holds me in dread, truth be told."

"I can imagine that being so," Bainbridge nodded,

genuinely sympathetic. "You have a brain in your skull, my dear, and a deep fear of letting it go to waste."

Victoria smiled softly.

"That sounds about right."

Bainbridge lowered himself into a chair and sat back.

"Well, if you are an apprentice detective now, you best take a look at that bit in the paper."

"Apprentice detective?"

"There is no other way for it," Bainbridge said solemnly. "You have to learn the trade."

Victoria did not argue. She was secretly delighted that Bainbridge was prepared to teach her all he knew. She had been afraid he would refuse to allow her into his world and would insist she went back to her mother. Ultimately, she would not have had a choice. She was terribly relieved he had agreed.

She turned her attention back to the article he had pointed out. As she read the few lines a frown puckered her brow.

"Do you have the same thoughts I do?" Bainbridge said.

Victoria opened her mouth and then hesitated.

"I am not sure."

"Let me give you my thoughts, then," Bainbridge replied. "Supposing Simon Underwood also boasts the nickname One-Foot, might we be looking at a motive for murder?"

"This legal fight?" Victoria said. "How would that work?"

"There are a couple of possibilities," Bainbridge said. "We might suppose someone did not want Simon to become a legal boxer for one. Or someone did not want him fighting this Mr Head."

"Or the name could be a coincidence."

"True," Bainbridge nodded. "But it is making these odd little connections that can be the key to resolving a case. I believe tomorrow we ought to seek out Mr Head and find out if he was due to fight One-Foot. It could be meaningless, a coincidence, that is all, or it could give us a new lead."

The frown eased on Victoria's face.

"If it leads us closer to his killer and saves Franklin's life, it has to be worth a shot."

"Precisely," Bainbridge said, feeling fired up once more.

"If you think it is urgent, we could go right away?" Victoria suggested.

Bainbridge looked at her in horror.

"My dear, that would mean missing dinner!"

Chapter Eleven

It was not until the following morning that they headed towards the offices listed in the newspaper advertisement, where tickets could be purchased for the prospective fight between Head and Underwood. They proved to be a semi-respectable set of rooms behind a greengrocer's shop. Notices pasted on a board outside the main door advertised an array of events, from a musical performance by a Greek songstress to a séance with an American medium. For each of these occasions tickets were limited and only available within the offices.

Bainbridge peered thoughtfully at a poster, a touch too vain to don his spectacles in public, so he almost pressed his nose against the image.

"The display of prestidigitation sounds intriguing," he said.

"What is prestidigitation?" Victoria frowned.

"It is the fanciful term for conjuring tricks, more commonly known as sleight of hand and performed on a regular basis, and rather skilfully I should say, by a number of the lowlier inhabitants of this fair city. Namely, they make things disappear without the owner realising, though some prefer to call this form of conjuring, pickpocketing."

Bainbridge smiled. Victoria had tipped her head on one side and was giving him a curious look.

"You have quite the head full of things, do you not?" she said.

"Is that a compliment?"

"It ought to be."

"Then I shall accept it as such," Bainbridge nodded, shall we go inside.

He opened the door and held it for Victoria. The office was a cramped little place of dark wood and green wallpaper. There was one solid and tall wood counter, behind which an older gentleman was perched on a high stool. Behind him was a selection of pigeonholes, presumably each containing details for the various performances the company organised.

"Good afternoon," the gentleman behind the desk said, lifting his head from some paperwork. "Welcome to Greene's Artistic Agency. We are the suppliers of the finest entertainment to this county, including a wealth of variety artists to suit all tastes and temperaments. Might I interest you in one of our summer brochures? It contains a complete listing of all our events through the next few months."

The gentleman had plucked up a paper brochure and passed it directly to Victoria who thanked him and started to scan through it.

"Oh dear, Julius, it says the tickets for the prestidigitation performance are sold out," she declared.

The gentleman behind the desk became crestfallen for them.

"That has been an extremely popular performance and due to the nature of the artistry a smaller audience is preferred, which has unfortunately resulted in the sale of all the tickets. Perhaps there is something else I might interest you in?"

Bainbridge played up to the moment.

"I had wondered about the boxing match you advertised," he said. "It was in the paper just the other day and I have never actually been to one."

"Oh my," the helpful assistant looked miserable, "oh my, I must inform you that the match has been postponed due to unforeseen circumstances."

"Really?" Bainbridge said, acting ruffled by the news. "First you have no tickets for the prestidigitation, now you tell me one of your other performances is postponed. I am starting to wonder about your professionalism."

The older gentleman looked aggrieved, as Bainbridge had intended.

"It is truly an unfortunate scenario utterly out of our control."

"Unforeseen circumstances," Bainbridge puffed, playing the unimpressed colonel to perfection. "A good way of saying nothing, if you ask me. Makes the whole company seem underhand. Tell me, do you ever actually host a performance?"

"Good sir, we are a genuine company and all I have stated has been sincere."

"What can be the bother with a boxing match?" Bainbridge blustered. "Is it the venue? The licensing? It is all legal, I suppose? It said as much in the newspaper, but anyone can say anything in the newspapers, they do it every day!"

Bainbridge waved his hands about demonstrating his indignation.

"Calm down Julius," Victoria said in the voice of someone who is used to enduring these demonstrations and did not take them seriously. "This gentleman is only doing his job."

"I don't trust a word of it," Bainbridge grumbled. "And that's a fact."

"Please, sir, it is a genuine circumstance," the unfortunate assistant said. "I have spent much of the morning refunding tickets. One of the fighters is no longer able to attend."

"Not Duncan Head?" Bainbridge gasped, grabbing the edge of the counter and looking horror struck. "He is not injured?"

"No sir, thankfully he is fully sound. It happens to be the other fellow who is no longer able to fight."

"That newcomer?" Bainbridge gave a snort. "Bad form, very bad form. How does he expect to succeed in the business if he does not even show up for his first match? His card will be marked, his career over before it began."

"I imagine the gentleman is not entirely concerned about that," the assistant said, now he was speaking he was becoming more vocal. "On account that he sadly passed away the other night."

Bainbridge paused in his fake bluster. It looked like he had been taken aback by the news and was reconsidering what he had just said. In reality, he was thinking that here was perfect confirmation that Simon Underwood was also Simon One-Foot. The odds of Underwood being a completely different street fighter who had also had the misfortune of dying two nights ago were too slim to be considered.

"That is truly shocking," Victoria said in a strangled voice. "The poor man cannot have been that old."

"No, madame," the assistant replied. "I believe he suffered an accident or such. It has caused quite a problem for us. But I must assure you that a match will be rescheduled for Mr Head as soon as we have a new, suitable fighter lined up for him."

"Terrible," Bainbridge sighed. "And just at the start of his boxing career."

"Rather unfortunate," the assistant agreed. "I am sure you appreciate why we have had to postpone things now?"

"I do," Bainbridge assured him. "Tragic, tragic."

"Might there be another performance I could interest you in?" the assistant asked brightly, hoping for a sale.

Victoria gave him a suspicious look.

"Have any others been cancelled, postponed or sold out?"

"Not currently," the assistant promised her. "Though I believe we are down to the last couple of tickets for the séance."

"I'll need time to consider," Bainbridge said. "I shall peruse the brochure at home."

"Of course, sir, and if it is more convenient, we are able to accept telegrammed orders for tickets. Many of our customers prefer that method for its speed and efficiency."

"Ah, very good!" Bainbridge said. "Good day!"

"Good day, sir, I hope it is a pleasant one for you."

They exited the office, Victoria idly thumbing through the brochure.

"I did not know you were quite the actor," she said without looking up.

Bainbridge stood a little taller.

"I was Hamlet in my old school's production of the great bard's play, and I was in the Army Amateur Dramatics Society," he said proudly. "Acting can prove useful in the work of a detective."

Victoria said nothing, a soft smile on her face.

"I believe our next stop should be to enquire after Mr White's health," Bainbridge said thoughtfully as they neared the car. "With any luck, he might be able to speak to us."

They drove back through the roads, the brochure now in Bainbridge's hands so he could peruse the contents.

"What on earth is water music? And how does one perform it?" Bainbridge frowned at the printed details of one performance.

"I could not tell you."

"Apparently it is extremely popular, as there are three performances for it in August alone."

"Perhaps we should attend it? Expand our minds to new knowledge?"

Bainbridge snorted to himself.

"I was more inclined towards the boxing."

They trundled down the road towards the ruins of Mr White's house. It was a sorry sight. Burned beyond salvation, the fire brigade had pulled down the roof and walls before they fell down, reducing it to a pile of soot-stained rubble.

Bainbridge looked upon the remains solemnly. A few scraps that had survived fire and water were all that remained to indicate that once this had been a home. Snippets of the past, of another life. Here were the charred pages of a book. There a picture frame, its contents lost. Fragments of Mr White's existence.

Bainbridge tutted to himself. The houses either side of the burned shell were in perilous condition too. It had been by sheer luck that the fire had not spread up to the attic of White's homes, else it would have had free rein along the entire row. The attics did not have dividing walls, a feature to save on construction materials and time, but which meant if fire crept into one, it could leap easily through all the rest.

Though the attics had been spared, the lower adjoining walls were badly burned and structurally impaired. Noticeably, on the right-hand house, the wall was significantly cracked, and efforts were being made by a team of workmen to shore it up with props.

Victoria brought the car to a stop outside the house where Mr White had been taken the previous day.

"I ought to discover how I put fuel in this thing," she said, gazing at the instrument panel of the car in a thoughtful fashion. "I have no idea how I tell when the tank is getting low."

Bainbridge was descending from the car, considering it none of his business how the thing worked. He was merely an observer in the bright new world of modern technology. They sauntered up to the house and knocked on the door. It was barely a moment before the younger woman from the day before opened it.

"Oh," she said, surprised to see them.

"We came to enquire about Mr White," Bainbridge said, removing his hat.

"The poor man," the woman sighed. "I don't think he

has long for this world."

She stepped back from the door.

"You can come see him, maybe a visit will cheer him."

She showed them into the front room where White was still tucked up on the inadequately sized sofa. A blanket was draped over his knees and a shawl around his shoulders, yet he shivered still, while beads of sweat poured down his forehead. He opened bleary, red eyes at the arrival of Bainbridge and Victoria.

"These are the kind people who raised the alarm yesterday," the younger woman told him. "They just came to see how you were doing."

Mr White stared blankly at Bainbridge.

"I need to get back to the stove," the woman told him. "You can let yourselves out when you are done. Try not to trouble him for too long."

She departed back to her chores. Victoria gave Bainbridge a look. He knew what she was thinking. Mr White looked as if he was already one foot in the grave, his mind certainly appeared to be on the other side already.

"Hello Mr White," he said. "How are you feeling?"

Mr White shivered and stared at him.

"It has been quite an upsetting few days for you," Bainbridge added. "I was sorry to hear about your friend's sudden demise."

White made no indication that this information had sunk in, there was something glazed about his stare as if he were looking straight through them.

"He is quite cracked," Victoria whispered to her uncle.

Bainbridge did not want to give up so easily on the man.

"We were coming to see you yesterday, concerning Simon," he said. "What happened to him was terrible and we wished to pass on our condolences. We have already spoken with Mr Stokes."

Still no response. Victoria shook her head. Bainbridge watched the man sweat and shiver, wondering how he was still alive at all. Perhaps, if his fever broke, there might be a chance for him, though there was no knowing what other damage his body might have suffered.

Mr White started to cough, tipping his head down and helplessly gagging. Dark phlegm was expelled onto the floor and Victoria made a noise of disgust.

"It is black!"

"He has inhaled a lot of soot," Bainbridge explained, before turning his attention back to Mr White. "Does that feel better?"

White ran a hand over his lips, then slumped back on the sofa. His eyes sank shut and he looked utterly exhausted. Bainbridge knew he could help them no more.

"Our apologies for disturbing you and we hope you are feeling better soon," he said politely, though it was unclear if any of this sank into the ailing man's consciousness. "Our best wishes for a full recovery."

Bainbridge nudged Victoria and they left the house.

"Do you think he is dying?" Victoria asked him as they approached the car.

"I do not particularly call that living," Bainbridge said, thinking about the wad of soot the man had coughed up. "I fear his lungs are done for."

Victoria was glum.

"What now?"

Bainbridge pulled his pocket watch from his waistcoat and assessed the time.

"I believe we should attend on the last of Simon Underwood's friends and see what he has to say. Hopefully, he has heard of Mr White's accident and will be inclined to speak to us a little more freely."

"What about Franklin? Ought we to see him and reassure him we are doing all we can?"

"I think we are of more use to him finding the real killer of Simon. If we cannot attend on him and say we have a solution and can restore his freedom, then I do not see we can benefit him by a visit at this stage. I do not wish to raise his hopes, only to dash them."

Victoria nodded.

"Yes, of course."

Bainbridge clambered back into the car while Victoria started the engine. The reluctance of the vehicle to begin concerned him and brought a frown of consternation to Victoria's face.

"I am even more worried than before that I might need fuel," Victoria said, placing one finger on her lower lip thoughtfully. "Where precisely does one get fuel for a car?"

Bainbridge hefted his shoulders.

"How should I know?"

Victoria stared at the car for quite some time before coming to a conclusion.

"Nothing else for it, we must purloin a carriage and find the nearest…" she fought for the right word, "car-stable and see what must be done."

"A hired carriage?" Bainbridge said. "Those things are expensive."

Victoria gave him a firm look.

"I shall not have my uncle walking places, it is not fitting," she said, jutting out her chin to show she meant it.

"Yes," Bainbridge sighed. "But you are not paying for the carriage!"

Chapter Twelve

Victoria found a carriage for hire, and then lost it again when she began asking the driver about places that sold fuel for cars. His views on the motorised vehicle were that it was the spawn of the Devil, designed to take work away from humble carriage drivers. If everyone had a car, there would be no need for carriages. What would happen to the horses? In short, he refused to transport people so clearly devoted to that new-fangled form of vehicle and he absolutely would not tell them where they could get fuel for it.

Victoria gave a long sigh and turned to Bainbridge who was doing his best not to laugh.

"I hardly think it is funny," she said, spotting his smirk.

"No, positively not," Bainbridge replied.

"The man was a luddite. The world moves on. We cannot spurn progress because it might mean old ways are lost."

"Progress is a bitter word when it prevents you from putting food on the table," Bainbridge reminded her.

Victoria did not look convinced.

"What now?" she asked despondently.

Bainbridge glanced at the ground.

"It appears we still have legs and feet. I propose we walk to see the last of Mr Underwood's associates."

"I don't find that amusing either," Victoria said, lifting her nose in a way that reminded Bainbridge far too much of her mother. "Still, if we must."

They sauntered off; Victoria very downcast that she no longer had an automobile to transport her about. She was so glum about the matter, Bainbridge felt it necessary to try to cheer her up.

"Houston was keen on the automobile, you know. He was of a similar mind to you that it was the way of the future."

"Houston was very forward thinking," Victoria said softly. "I wish I had got to know him better, but mother was so against him."

"Your mother considered him a bad influence upon me," Bainbridge reflected. "Perhaps she thought he would be a bad influence upon you too?"

"And yet, despite her efforts, here I am pretending to be a detective."

"I would say you are doing better than merely pretending," Bainbridge consoled her.

Victoria brightened a little at this.

They turned down another street and after a half hour of walking they found themselves at the address of Mr Ottoman, the final companion of the unfortunate Simon Underwood. Unlike the other residences where they had found Stokes and White, Mr Ottoman's address was not a residential address, it was a shop that sold ironmongery, household cleaning supplies and, according to a poster in the window, 'Arsokill, the most effective pest poison on the market! Harmless to you, lethal to pests!'.

Bainbridge observed the display for Arsokill curiously. There was a dead stuffed rat lying before a tin of the stuff for good effect. He gave a shudder.

"Poisons always gives me the chills," he said. "Seen too

many accidental deaths that way."

Victoria was not listening to him.

"Mr Ottoman owns the shop," she pointed to the signage above the door which indicated the proprietor of the establishment was one Mr H. Ottoman. "I did not expect that, after the others."

"I endeavour to not expect anything," Bainbridge said haughtily, though he had actually expected another rundown rented set of rooms. He had been impressed that Mr White had a whole house to himself. "A good detective keeps his, or her, mind open."

Victoria gave him a look that suggested she did not believe a word of what he had just said, then she opened the door to the shop and let herself in. Bainbridge was taken by surprise and was flustered he had not been able to open the door for her, which was the polite and proper way of things. Instead, he found himself trailing behind his niece as she sauntered into Mr Ottoman's intriguing emporium.

"Good morning, Madame. Sir," a gentleman in a long brown shop coat greeted them from behind a counter.

"Good morning," Victoria replied. "I assume you are Mr Ottoman?"

"Ah, you saw my name outside! Yes, this is my humble establishment," the shopkeeper smiled.

Bainbridge took a good look at the man. His surname had suggested he might be of European origins, namely Prussian, or possibly Bavaria. Certainly that region, at least. However, Mr Ottoman's solid Norfolk accent and ruddy complexion implied his family had been settled in the county at least for most of his life, if not before.

"I am Colonel Bainbridge," Bainbridge explained himself. "This is my niece, Victoria. We have come about a very delicate matter."

Mr Ottoman was not alarmed by this statement. His salesman's smile was plastered on his face and he was ready for anything.

"Indeed, indeed," he grinned. "Is it about door

furniture? I find that often is a trying issue for people?"

"Not door furniture, no," Bainbridge said. "We have come concerning the unfortunate demise of Simon Underwood."

Mr Ottoman stiffened; his smile became a little fixed. Perhaps it was because Bainbridge had used Simon's correct name rather than his alias that caused Ottoman to glance at his shop door. He cleared his throat.

"I don't know why you would come to me."

"Mr Underwood perished the night before last and due to the testimony of yourself and your friends, Stokes and White, a friend of ours has had the misfortune of being arrested and charged with murder," Bainbridge continued. "A matter, you will understand, that we are deeply concerned about."

Mr Ottoman had gone a fraction pale, but he brazened out the accusation.

"I do not recall accusing anyone of anything," he said lightly.

"And yet the police have the notion that Mr Underwood was killed due to a lethal punch swung by Franklin Ward. I believe we both can agree that Franklin swung no such blow, in fact, he was no better than a punching bag for your friend."

Ottoman nervously cleared his throat again and they could feel him willing the shop door to open and admit another customer.

"I cannot say I recall any of this matter," he said, with a cheerful smile.

"You are denying saying any of it?" Victoria said, appalled.

"I suppose I am," Ottoman was back in his stride. "Now, if there was nothing else?"

Bainbridge marched forward and thumped his hand on the counter.

"Good heavens man! Your actions have placed an innocent in danger of being tried for murder! Do you not have a conscience?"

Ottoman looked unsettled, but he was not so shaken as to be convinced to admit anything.

"I cannot help that the police have got the wrong end of the stick," he said lightly. "The police are like that, you know."

Bainbridge was going to say something further, until Victoria marched forward and slapped both hands down on the counter and leaned towards the shopkeeper. The sudden move threw him off-guard a fraction. It was not the sort of thing you expected from a well-dressed lady.

"Look here, you," Victoria growled at him. "I have walked – walked – over a mile to get here and talk to you. My feet hurt because these shoes do not suit walking and I am hot and bothered in a way I very much dislike. Now, I did not put myself to such discomfort to be fobbed off with lies, so you better start speaking the truth before I make you wish you had never seen door furniture before in your life!"

Ottoman opened his mouth, then he frowned and looked at Bainbridge.

"What does that mean?"

Bainbridge was rather astonished by his niece's sudden deportment, and also mildly impressed.

"I believe she means she will cause you some harm with a door knocker, or such," he told Ottoman.

"Oh," Ottoman considered. "That's rather unkind."

"You are being unkind, Mr Ottoman," Victoria pointed a finger at him. "Consider Franklin Ward who should, by all rights, be back at Mr Flint's pub doing his daily chores, not locked in a prison cell wondering what his fate might be."

Ottoman blinked at her but did not speak.

"My interpretation of events," Bainbridge said to the shopkeeper, "is that the late Simon Underwood was brought to his demise by the hand of someone you are afraid of or have some connection to that is too important for you to implicate them in this crime. Thus, you found yourself a scapegoat in the form of Franklin Ward, and it might have worked for you, except I now know that Simon Underwood was not killed at the place he fought Franklin. In fact, it was some distance away and a witness saw it all. The event was nothing like you told the police, and with this new evidence we shall have Franklin freed, while you will find yourself answering some difficult questions."

Ottoman swallowed down on his anxiety, his gaze flicking between them.

"I don't think you appreciate the situation," he said.

"I fear that most likely," Bainbridge assured him. "Yet, that does not change anything."

"Mr White has clearly been deeply upset by events," Victoria added, lightening her tone.

Ottoman turned to her sharply.

"What do you mean?"

"Have you not heard?" Victoria asked innocently.

Ottoman looked very worried now.

"What should I have heard?"

The look of horror on his face for a moment quelled the outrage of Victoria and Bainbridge. It was the colonel who gently broke the news to him.

"Mr White was caught up in a house fire yesterday and I fear he shall not recover."

"I do not understand," Ottoman looked panicked. "What fire?"

"It appears he drunk himself into a stupor and then his lit pipe tumbled to the floor where it set the rug aflame and was fuelled by the spilt alcohol all about," Bainbridge explained.

Ottoman's eyes widened and his fingers gripped hard to the edge of his counter.

"White did not drink!" he declared.

"He was found surrounded by bottles of gin," Victoria told him gently. "The fire nearly took out the whole street."

"No, White never drank! He had taken a pledge!" Ottoman declared. "Simon ribbed him about it all the time, but he would not be swayed. He used to be a devil when he had a drink in him, that's why he stopped."

Ottoman's eyes had grown teary as the news sunk in.
"He wouldn't."

"Possibly the shock of everything and the guilt of implicating an innocent man in the crime tipped him back into the bottle," Bainbridge suggested. "He would not be the first."

Ottoman wiped the back of his hands over his eyes.

"You say he is done for?"

"It looks likely," Bainbridge said sympathetically. "I am sorry."

Ottoman was dazed by the news. Two friends lost in the space of two days, it was hard to fathom and only the other night they had been on the up, celebrating a better future ahead.

"Might I say," Victoria added. "You do not strike me as someone who would be a companion to an illegal street fighter."

Bainbridge wanted to give her a sharp nudge for that. He had just thought they were getting somewhere and now she had put the man's back up.

"What does that mean?" Ottoman asked.

"I believe I was fairly clear in the statement," Victoria said. "You strike me as a respectable sort of man, running his own business successfully. Not the sort to hang around with someone who could get him into trouble."

Ottoman pulled himself upright and looked offended.

"Simon was my oldest friend. We knew each other from school. Our paths had diverged over the years, but that did not change our friendship."

"For such an old friend, you felt no qualms in giving a false name for his murderer," Bainbridge muttered.

Ottoman tried to look righteously indignant, but they both knew the statement was accurate.

"I do not want to talk to you anymore," the shopkeeper declared.

"You might not, but we have not finished with you," Victoria said firmly.

Ottoman glared at her.

"You cannot interrogate me in my own shop, I shall not stand for it!"

Victoria crossed her arms over her chest and glowered at him, daring him to do more. Ottoman had nothing much to back up his outrage except for more sharp words.

"I told no lies to the police and that is for sure," he said. "I cannot vouch for what others might have said. I merely mentioned that Simon had a spat with Mr Ward that evening."

"You allowed the police to suppose that Franklin was the killer," Bainbridge snorted.

"I cannot help what policemen think," Ottoman said firmly.

Bainbridge could see they were going to get nowhere with him. He was determined to bring them round in continuous circles.

"You are a disappointment to me, Mr Ottoman," he said.

"Because I will not play your games?" the shopkeeper retorted.

"No, because for a man who claims to be deeply affected by his friend's demise, you are utterly uninterested in bringing his real killer to justice. Either out of fear or out of selfishness, you shall not speak the truth and so you are no friend to Simon Underwood."

"I resent that!" Ottoman snapped.

"Perhaps you do," Bainbridge sighed. "I wonder if Simon Underwood, should his soul be in heaven listening down, resents that his friends have so abandoned him."

"He is not abandoned!" Ottoman protested.

"You continue to tell yourself that," Bainbridge shrugged. "Perhaps you will sleep better for it."

Ottoman had flushed red, anger and guilt mingling into a heady mix. Bainbridge knew it was time for them to go. He tried to catch Victoria's eye, but she was too busy glaring at Ottoman.

"In case you change your mind and consider telling the truth, you may find me here," Bainbridge produced a business card from his pocket and flicked it onto the counter. "Remember, when the police are hounding you for the truth, that I made you an offer and was prepared to help you. Instead, you turned me down."

Ottoman was scowling at the card as if it were something dirty. He refused to touch it.

"Very well, Mr Ottoman, you cannot say we did not try."

Bainbridge lightly touched Victoria's arm and motioned to the door. They left together, the fresh air a relief after the tension within the shop.

"I thought he would talk to us," Victoria looked glum.

Bainbridge smiled at her.

"He might, eventually," he said. "But we have to look at things from a new angle now. If Simon's friends are so adamant they shall not tell the truth, then we must try other means. I believe it is time we took a deeper look into Underwood's world, beginning with his home. Perhaps there we shall find a clue to this mystery and why someone would rush up to him in the dark and attack him."

"Maybe it was someone who had lost a fight to him," Victoria grumbled.

"Maybe," Bainbridge agreed. "I suspect it shall be something like that."

Chapter Thirteen

They did not have the address for Simon Underwood's home and with the car temporarily out of action, they agreed to make their way to the police station and request assistance from Inspector Dougal. It was just after lunch when they arrived, and Bainbridge was feeling the gripes of hunger in his belly. Desk Sergeant Greaves gave them a friendly nod as they entered.

"The Inspector is out," he informed them.

"Oh," Victoria said in such a despondent fashion that Greaves was quite upset he had caused her distress.

"He won't be long, I reckon. He is after a man about a pig."

"Pigs is it now?" Bainbridge said, rubbing the small moustache over his upper lip.

"Stolen pigs," Greaves added. "Or possibly just mislaid, it is hard to tell."

"How often are pigs mislaid?" Victoria asked.

"You would be surprised," Greaves said solemnly. "Now, might I help you at all while you wait?"

"My car has run out of fuel," Victoria said swiftly.

"What sort of fuel?" Greaves asked, thinking about the coal in the scuttle by the fireplace of the constables' sitting room.

"I have absolutely no idea," Victoria replied. "Sven never mentioned."

"Sven?" Greaves frowned.

"She acquired the car from him," Bainbridge said, glancing at Victoria. "Though I still have misgivings about that."

Victoria bluntly ignored him.

"There must be someone in this city who knows about these things," she said to Greaves.

He tapped his chin.

"I reckon I could send a messenger out to find someone," he suggested.

"That would be most appreciated," Victoria smiled.

It was the sort of smile that men would fight to have shine upon them, and it had a suitable effect on Greaves who went into action at once, rounding up a young constable to send on the errand.

In the meantime, Bainbridge sat down on one of the hard wooden chairs in the waiting area of the police station and wished it were not improper to take his shoes off in public.

"I did say about all that walking," Victoria remarked as she sat beside him.

"My doctor informs me I should get more exercise," Bainbridge countered. "Though he also tells me to lose weight and I think that a load of nonsense. Older people need a little extra to have something to lose should they be taken ill."

Victoria frowned as she tried to follow his logic.

"Still, once I have a better idea of how to refuel the car, this shall not happen again," she said happily.

Bainbridge settled back in the chair and shut his eyes, trying to ignore his rumbling belly. Lose weight, when his stomach acted most of the time as if his throat had been cut? What poppycock!

"At least we can inform the inspector that it could not possibly be Franklin who killed Mr Underwood and he shall be released," Victoria continued.

Bainbridge opened his eyes and attempted not to sigh. This was going to require some explaining.

"The situation may not be as simple as that," he said.

"Whyever not? We know that Mr Underwood was attacked in a completely different place to where he fought Franklin."

"Yes, but we do not have evidence to prove that Franklin was not the one to attack him. He could have followed Underwood to take his revenge."

"You are not saying you believe that?" Victoria asked, appalled.

"No, I am not," Bainbridge blustered, annoyed she had thought he was doubting Franklin. Was she not the one who had told him not to be so quick to consider Franklin innocent? "My point is that from the perspective of a judge and jury, should matters go to court, there is no absolute proof of Franklin's innocence, and three men have claimed he was responsible."

"They lied about where it happened," Victoria added. "You cannot trust liars."

"True," Bainbridge gave her that. "But Franklin is unable to elaborate on his movements that evening, due to his head injuries and so even with the lies told, he remains a potential suspect."

Victoria pouted at this news.

"I really did not like that Mr Ottoman. Nor Mr Stokes for that matter. They were sly and secretive. I could imagine them doing in their friend and then laying the blame on Franklin."

Bainbridge straightened up as she said this, his mind going over the possibility. Then he shook his head. No, their witness had seen a fourth man, it was not likely to be one of Simon's cronies. Though, guilt over killing Simon could be the reason White went on a drinking binge and nearly burned himself to death.

"I do not think they killed him," he said.

Victoria looked glum.

"What happens if we cannot figure this out?" she asked Bainbridge.

"That is not an option," he told her.

"But if we cannot get people to be honest and tell us the truth…"

"We shall find another way," Bainbridge said firmly, cutting her off.

Victoria was not convinced, but she decided it was best not to say more. They both fell into contemplative silence, until the inspector arrived.

"Hello Bainbridge, Miss Bovington."

Inspector Dougal looked quite spritely and clean for someone who had been tracking down stray pigs.

"How are you getting on?"

"The usual. A little progress, but not enough," Bainbridge answered. "Might we bother you a moment?"

"Come up to the office," Dougal told him. "I would like to hear your thoughts on this matter."

They were soon in his office explaining their eventful couple of days. Dougal was intrigued by the witness' description of the assault in Cattle Market Row, and troubled by the fire that looked likely to snatch Mr White from this world sooner rather than later. He scratched his chin as he considered all this information.

"I feel like there should be a pattern to it all," he said. "But I'll be damned if I can see. Oh, apologies dear lady."

Victoria gave him an innocent look.

"Apologies for what?"

Dougal cleared his throat and turned his attention back to Bainbridge.

"It is news to me that Underwood was looking to become a legitimate boxer. I thought he was the kind who would never give up street fighting."

"I think we both can agree the two were not exclusive and the chances were Underwood would continue his illegal brawling."

"Yes, but if he started to do well on the boxing circuit, then it would be prudent to avoid the scandal street fighting could bring."

"If," Bainbridge said with emphasis.

"Excuse me for being slightly ill-educated on the subject, but what is the different between a boxing match and an illegal street fight?" Victoria asked.

"The gambling, mainly," Dougal explained. "At an organised boxing match there is technically gambling, but it is regulated and controlled. At a street fight, anything goes."

"Same applies to the style of fighting," Bainbridge added. "A boxing match has rounds and a referee. There are rules about where you can punch a person and you cannot bite or kick. There is none of that in street fighting. It is far more brutal."

"The sort of people who choose to go to a street fight want to see blood and someone being pretty badly mangle," Dougal shuddered. "They bet on all sorts of things, even on the survival of an opponent. It is a nasty sport, and it is my job to stop it, but, of course, the fight organisers are aware of that and move their venues all the time. They advertise by word of mouth and it is only through luck that we can track a fight down."

"I am starting to dislike this Simon Underwood," Victoria said. "He sounds quite a brute. Not that I thought greatly of him after how he treated Franklin."

"I suppose you do not know of a connection between Jimmy Black and Underwood?" Bainbridge asked the inspector.

"Black is involved in street fighting. He runs gambling operations for it. That would connect him to Underwood, why do you ask?"

"The night he died, Underwood spotted Jimmy Black in the pub he was stirring up trouble in and decided to leave. I wondered if there was more to it than simply thinking it was prudent not to cause a fight in the place a man like Black is quietly drinking."

"I cannot offer you anything," Dougal shrugged. "I had not heard of trouble between them, but then I would be unlikely to hear much about them at all."

"None of this helps Franklin," Victoria said miserably.

"Not at face value, no," Dougal admitted. "But it offers a line of defence, casting doubt on him as the attacker. Such a shame no further witnesses have come forward concerning that night."

"I hoped to take a look around Mr Underwood's home to see if there was anything there that could throw light on the situation," Bainbridge said. "We do not happen to have the address."

Dougal gestured for the piece of paper he had given them earlier and then wrote a new address on it.

"You will need this too," he opened a drawer and produced a key for them. "We went to his home to secure it after he was reported dead to us. We did not search it, as at that point we had three witnesses telling us who had committed the crime and no reason to doubt them."

"We shall take a closer look," Bainbridge said, taking the key.

"I have not forgotten about other matters, Bainbridge," Dougal said as they stood to leave.

Bainbridge paused; this was not a subject he wanted brought up.

"I am still investigating what happened to Houston," Dougal added.

"Do you have any leads upon that?" Victoria asked him. "It was such a terrible thing."

Bainbridge wished she would not ask, talking about the matter stirred up his grief and he saw no value to it, not when it was not assisting them to find a solution.

"I am striving hard," Dougal assured Victoria. "I will find an answer."

"You are most kind," Bainbridge told him and then headed for the door swiftly before they went into a full discussion about Houston's death. He was not in the mood for that.

Victoria followed him downstairs slowly. As he reached the bottom, he stopped and turned to her.

"I can feel your disapproval through the back of my jacket."

"Disapproval?" Victoria said with round innocent eyes.

"You think I should have had a hearty discussion about Houston's murder with the inspector," Bainbridge blustered, the words falling out of his mouth fast. "You think we should have compared notes or something."

Victoria gave him a sad, sympathetic look and it was worse than her questions. He turned away sharply and would have liked to have left the station, except Victoria quickly caught him up and placed her hand on his sleeve.

"I was not thinking that," she promised him.

Bainbridge did not want to meet her eyes.

"I think I do not understand a fraction of what Houston meant to you," Victoria added. "Perhaps I shall never understand, but I would like to try and if you ever want to talk…"

"I do not," Bainbridge said firmly, pulling his arm away.

"Very good," Victoria told him. "Because I was not going to offer to do the listening. I hate people laying their woes upon my shoulders. Keep it all bottled up, that is what I say."

Bainbridge turned to face her and saw the look on her face.

"Sarcasm," he said.

"I know," Victoria responded. "I am terrible for it. I simply cannot help myself."

Bainbridge sighed.

"Look, I am not someone who talks about their emotions. It is not how I was raised. Your mother would understand."

"That is because Mother rarely has an original emotion," Victoria said cynically. "Caring about another person for their sake alone would be novel to her."

"That sounded slightly bitter," Bainbridge said, his own concerns cast aside for the moment.

Victoria shrugged at him.

"We cannot choose our parents. I suppose that could be argued a curse and a blessing."

"You know, one day you shall have to reconcile with your Mother," Bainbridge said gently.

"Can we not talk about it?" Victoria said in exasperation. "I wonder if that constable has found some fuel for my car yet?"

"I may not see eye-to-eye with your mother," Bainbridge persisted. "But she is not a bad person and she must be worried about you."

"Worried about any scandal I might bring upon her, you mean?" Victoria sniffed.

"No, I mean she must be worried about you. You did send her a message to let her know where you were?"

"Of course I did," Victoria grumbled. "I am not callous."

She stormed off towards Greaves behind his desk. Bainbridge was not convinced he believed her.

"Any news about my car?" Victoria asked the desk sergeant.

"I have a constable on it, madame," Greaves smiled. "He went to fetch the vehicle."

"Thank goodness for that, I cannot walk a step further," Victoria leaned rather heavily on the counter, lifting one protesting foot. "I was not designed for walking."

Greaves was fussing over her, suggesting he make her a cup of tea while she waited. Bainbridge walked to the doors of the station and looked through a window out to the road beyond. He had not been lying to Victoria when he said he would find a way to solve this mystery. He would not let Franklin down, the problem was, he was rather stumped on what he could precisely do. He was relying heavily on finding a clue at Simon Underwood's home, something that might indicate why the man had been assaulted. It was unlikely the intention of the attack was to kill Simon, that had been sheer bad luck. No, someone had wished to scare him, or take revenge. Maybe a street fight had ended badly, and someone was now looking for vengeance? But why had Underwood's companions been so determined to lie about it? Could it be they didn't actually know who was responsible?

Bainbridge allowed this idea to take form. It had been a dark night. The attacker had come up behind them, struck and raced off. Perhaps they never got a good look at him, perhaps, when the police started asking questions, to get them off their backs they gave the name of Franklin because they simply had no idea who the real attacker was? As this notion took hold, a new pit of despair slowly opened in Bainbridge's belly, for if Underwood's friends did not know the identity of the assailant, how was Bainbridge supposed to discover it?

It was a terrible thought and one he was not going to share with Victoria. He had promised he would find the person responsible for killing Underwood so that Franklin would be spared, and he kept his promises.

He was just not very sure how in this instance he was going to achieve that.

Chapter Fourteen

The car was duly refuelled by a man from a local engineering firm who knew about cars. Victoria pestered him for information on how to perform the procedure herself in the future and though he was obviously reluctant to explain the process to a woman, her persistence proved his downfall. With this new knowledge secured, Victoria felt content to clamber back into the car feeling smug that she could now look after the car herself. Bainbridge levered himself up beside her, wondering why they had to make the damn things so high.

"Where do we go?" Victoria asked, donning a giant pair of goggles to protect her eyes from dust and insects as they went along.

Bainbridge started to discuss a route to Underwood's home when he noticed the goggles.

"Are they necessary?"

"High speed motoring is a serious business. I must protect my eyes."

"Oh," Bainbridge considered this. "Ought I to have a pair too?"

"Oh no," Victoria said amused at his suggestion. "You are only a passenger."

Bainbridge was not entirely sure how to take that remark.

They pulled away from the path and Bainbridge began to direct them to the address. It was a nice day to just sit in a car and rest. Bainbridge could almost feel quite dopey as he warmed in his seat. He wouldn't mind dozing off. But then he glanced over and saw the tobacconist that Houston favoured, and his good humour was gone, replaced by that nasty hollow feeling in his stomach. A feeling he feared would never be gone. How could you ever come to terms with losing someone who had been so fundamental to your life? Bainbridge had always felt better about himself, about the world when he was in Houston's presence, now that was gone, and it seemed as if all he saw about him was bleakness and despair. He rather wanted to go home and shut himself up in his study and never, ever come out again.

"You have gone very quiet," Victoria said gently.

Bainbridge cleared his throat. It was tight and dry.

"I... hm."

Victoria was watching him out of the corner of her eye. She could make a fair guess at what was bothering him.

"It comes over you quite unexpected, grief," she said.

Bainbridge did not look her way.

"It is understandable, you know. I will gladly listen if you wish to talk about it," she added.

"What is there to say? Houston is dead and there is nothing I can do about it."

Victoria did not answer him until she had negotiated a tight corner.

"We can talk about how you are feeling."

"I do not talk about that," Bainbridge sniffed. "I shall be fine."

Victoria gave him a sideways look that was altogether too knowing. Bainbridge shifted uncomfortably in his seat.

"I know it is not what people are supposed to do, talk about their feelings," she said. "Yet, I rather fancy that is more for the benefit of the listener than for the person unburdening themselves. I think we assume others will be embarrassed or inconvenienced by our emotions, should we speak of them, and so we shy away from doing so. I read this article which said it was not healthy."

"People are always writing nonsense about the way people should or should not think," Bainbridge snorted.

"It need not be nonsense," Victoria countered.

"It might as well be," Bainbridge huffed. "Anyway, I am perfectly fine."

He was endeavouring to ignore the knot in his stomach and the tightness in his chest that was saying otherwise. Victoria did not continue the argument; she knew when she was battling a lost cause. She just had to hope that with time and patience, Bainbridge might be convinced to open up a little. There was a lot he had bottled up inside and she followed the modern line of thought that talking was the best therapy. Bainbridge had so much screwed up inside him that he would need to do a lot of talking to get it all out. She was determined to help him.

"I believe this is the house," Bainbridge said sharply as they trundled past a red-brick building.

Victoria battled with levers to bring the car to a stop and they both looked back at the property.

It was an older style three storey house, built probably a hundred years ago. It had seen better days and the roof was in need of a few tiles. Victoria was starting to get a feel for the places that their witnesses and victim lived in, she was no longer surprised by the sight of the house.

They descended from the car and walked across the road to the front door.

"Dare I ask, how much of this property does Mr Underwood reside in?" Victoria said as she observed the peeling paint of the door.

"I believe he has the attic space, from what Inspector Dougal has written down on this paper," Bainbridge answered.

He rapped firmly on the door.

"I never realised how few people had a whole house to themselves until today," Victoria reflected. "It is quite the revelation."

The door shot open and a fearsome woman with fiery red hair and the glare of Medusa scowled at them.

"Yes?" she demanded.

"We have permission from Inspector Dougal to take a look around the late Mr Underwood's rooms," Bainbridge said with delicate politeness.

Victoria was wrinkling her nose at the woman, having already taken a dislike to her.

"Why do you want to do that, then?" the woman glowered at Bainbridge.

"Madame," Bainbridge said calmly, "I am not at liberty to divulge that information, but I feel it prudent to inform you that the sooner I have had an opportunity to investigate the rooms, the sooner the police will be able to return to you the key to them so you might begin letting them out once more. I am sure you are feeling the pinch of being deprived of the income such rooms might afford you."

The woman had not entirely followed his speech, but she had latched on to the words 'income' and 'sooner'. She came to a snap decision.

"If letting some nosey busybodies look in those rooms gets the police out of my hair, go ahead. I am owed two weeks by Underwood as it is."

She stood back to let them in, catching a look at Victoria's face in the process.

"What are you so sour about?" she snapped.

Victoria turned to face her, Bainbridge wanted to nudge her and whisper to not cause trouble, but it was too late.

"Are you aware that the average frown uses considerably more muscles and places more strain on the face than a smile," Victoria said. "It is my duty, as a fellow member of the fairer sex to inform you that such behaviour ages you faster and creates deep, unmoving wrinkles."

The fiery woman had not expected this, and her mouth

dropped open as she tried to think of a suitable retort.

"Do not thank me," Victoria said, holding up a hand to stop her speaking. "As I said, it was my duty to tell you. I shall not have it on my conscience that a fellow woman has had her good looks ruined due to my inability to speak up."

With that Victoria headed for the staircase. Bainbridge was chuckling to himself as he followed. The woman was left stood behind, utterly perplexed. She massaged her forehead, feeling for those ominous lines Victoria had mentioned, then dashed away to try and find a mirror.

"Not bad," Bainbridge complimented his niece as they headed up to the attic.

Victoria offered him a smile.

"I believe I am learning."

"You are, indeed."

The door to the attic was locked, as they had known it would be. Bainbridge had the key from the inspector and rattled it in the lock. They entered a dark, narrow hallway with a pair of doors facing one another either side of them. Bainbridge did not precisely know what he was looking for, so it was as prudent to go left as it was to go right. Walking through the door they found themselves in Simon's bedroom. A brass bed was shoved beneath the dormer window and covered by a thin blanket, there were no curtains at the window, but then it was unlikely anyone was going to look in up here. A screen across one corner failed to hide a battered washstand with a jug and cracked mirror. The room smelt vaguely of the activities of a tomcat.

"What do you think we should look for?" Victoria asked, taking in the aspect of the room with a critical eye. "The ceiling is in desperate need of some paint."

"I have no firm idea of what will constitute a clue. In general, I work on the theory that one will know it when one sees it."

Victoria frowned then set about opening a trunk pressed into a corner. It seemed to mainly contain clothes. Bainbridge examined the bed, bending down stiffly to look underneath. Aside from a stray spider who he disturbed as he dropped to one knee, there was nothing of interest.

"Mr Underwood would have benefited from a better laundress," Victoria observed, pulling a stained pair of trousers from the trunk. "I have a nasty suspicion this is blood."

"Underwood was a street fighter," Bainbridge reminded her. "It's a messy business."

Victoria unpacked two pairs of trousers and three shirts, a waistcoat, a spare pair of braces and a jacket with one elbow worn through. She piled these onto the floor as she went.

Bainbridge had gone behind the screen to examine Underwood's more personal items. Bainbridge thought you learned a lot from a man by the way he shaved. He noted a cutthroat razor on the stand that was severely tarnished with rust. Not the sort of device he would bring anywhere near his face, for fear of catching something. Underwood apparently did not have the same concerns.

Beneath the washstand was a small box that contained quite the collection of digestive powders, purges, and pills for either firming up or loosening the motion of the bowels. It seemed Underwood had been suffering for a while with stomach gripes and had collected quite an array of cheap remedies to attempt to cure it.

"A man on borrowed time," Bainbridge muttered to himself.

"Do you think these are important?" Victoria called out.

Bainbridge emerged from behind the screen and walked over to where she had largely emptied the trunk.

"I believe these are betting slips," she said, handing him some crumpled papers.

"They are indeed," Bainbridge said, shuffling the papers in his hand. "More to the point, it appears Mr Underwood was betting on himself."

"Is that not bad form?" Victoria said.

"It is, and the sort of thing that can cause a lot of trouble. Though it is curious to see that Underwood was betting that he would win."

"Why is that curious?"

"Generally, when a person bets on their own performance, they bet they shall lose as that is easier to manufacture. They throw a match on purpose and earn their reward. Betting you will win is slightly riskier. You can guarantee a lose, you cannot guarantee a win."

"He would get in a lot of trouble for this," Victoria added.

"Oh yes, if anyone was to realise. I imagine he had one of his cronies place these bets on his behalf."

"No sign of any money," Victoria said. "If he was fixing matches to make money, why could he not afford to pay his landlady?"

"Why indeed," Bainbridge pocketed the betting slips. "And could this have been a motive for his attack?"

Having thoroughly searched the bedroom, they headed across the hallway to the second room, which was a sort of sitting area. There was a tatty sofa, which was close to collapsing to the floor and a fireplace with a kettle resting in the ashes of the grate. This room smelled like frying food, particularly bacon and cabbage. No doubt Underwood had performed some crude cookery upon the fireplace when he was hungry for his supper. There was a table shoved against a wall and upon it were a stack of magazines and posters. Victoria picked up one.

"It's about a prize fight," she said. "An advert for a match."

The next item in the pile was a sporting magazine, a cheap print that showed a crudely drawn boxer on the front. Each magazine beneath it was of a similar nature, there were also several loose papers that had been ripped from magazines and were articles concerning a recent match.

"I think it is safe to say that Mr Underwood had ambitions," Bainbridge picked up a poster for a prize fight. "He was not inclined to remain a street brawler all his days."

"I wonder how he made the transition?" Victoria was tidying the papers back up. "I assume you do not just wander up to a regular boxer and declare you want to fight them?"

"Someone must have either seen him fighting, such as a scout for a boxing agent, or he had someone help him," Bainbridge replied.

He had his hand down the cushions of the sofa looking for money or more tickets. According to the slips Victoria had found, Underwood had made a decent living betting on himself. He would have made an even better income if he had betted on losing, but it appeared Underwood was too proud to throw a match. Even so, there should have been a reasonable amount of money somewhere in the rooms, unless someone had been here before them and removed it.

Victoria opened an old biscuit tin and produced more betting slips.

"He did not just bet on himself," she said. "And he lost a lot."

She showed Bainbridge the slips, many of which had been scrawled across in fury, the results of the matches listed on them all.

"Underwood was taking his gambling seriously, trying to work out the form of his fellow boxers," Bainbridge said. "One might almost say he was trying to make gambling his profession."

"He was not very good at it," Victoria sniffed. "Do you think these are important?"

"I am not sure," Bainbridge admitted. "We might take them anyway."

The rooms did not offer much else in the way of clues. There were no obvious threats or indications of someone having a grudge against Underwood. The betting slips were all they had.

"What now?" Victoria asked as Bainbridge lowered himself onto the sofa.

"I need to think," he said. "Perhaps at home."

He was just contemplating the complicated procedure of extracting himself from the sofa when they both heard a noise on the stairs. It sounded like the fall of a foot.

Then someone opened the door.

Chapter Fifteen

Victoria gave Bainbridge an alarmed look, trying to ask with her eyes what they should do. Bainbridge calmly lifted his hand to indicate they should wait. In his long experience, it was never wise to rush these things.

Whoever had entered the attic was stood just within the hallway, silent and unmoving. Victoria was getting twitchy. Bainbridge held up his hand again and tried to look stern, as if that might help. Victoria was ignoring him and starting to lean sideways to try to peer through the door. Bainbridge, unable to speak, did his best to articulate with silent and elaborate movements of his lips that she ought to remain right where she was.

The person outside was moving again, heading away from them towards the bedroom. Bainbridge relaxed, thinking now would be a good time for them to slip away. Then the footsteps stopped, the person spun on their heel and marched straight into the sitting room.

Victoria, since she was standing up, was the first person they saw. She gave a little pretend start and clasped a hand to her chest as if she had been unaware of the intruder's presence.

"Mr Ottoman! Whatever are you doing here?"

Ottoman had a look of utter surprise on his face as he looked from her, to Bainbridge still happily ensconced on the sofa. Bainbridge was in no rush to get up. Despite its appearance, the aging couch was quite comfortable.

"I could ask you the same!" Ottoman blustered back, but the pause before his response made it seem more of an afterthought and it didn't have much force.

"We have permission from Inspector Dougal to be here," Bainbridge informed him. "Do you?"

Ottoman clearly wanted to say he did, but he knew that was not going to get him far, so he fell silent.

"That is what I thought," Bainbridge said, dragging himself from the sofa with a groan of effort. "What has brought you here so urgently?"

Ottoman crossed his arms over his chest.

"I don't have to speak to you."

He stuck out his chin defiantly.

"I imagine he was after those betting slips we found," Victoria said to her uncle in a loud aside. "They had not been claimed yet."

"Ah, yes. It would make sense that one of Simon's compatriots was placing and claiming the bets for him."

Ottoman scowled at them.

"That is none of your business," he declared. "You ought to hand them over!"

"It seems to me, Mr Ottoman, that those slips could be important for other reasons. If someone discovered Underwood was betting on himself, it could be motive for his assault."

"I already told the police who did that and why," Ottoman protested.

"You lied," Victoria pointed a rebuking finger at him. "Did your mother not teach you what happens to liars?"

Ottoman was not impressed.

"You need to give me those slips!"

"They are evidence," Bainbridge stated haughtily,

though he could not say for certain if that was accurate. They might have nothing to do with the case at hand.

"Evidence?" Ottoman glared. "They are none of your business!"

"Then whose business might they be?" Victoria asked him. "Perhaps Jimmy Black would be interested in them?"

Ottoman blanched at the man's name, which was exactly what Victoria had intended. He recovered swiftly.

"Mr Black has nothing to do with those slips. They did him no harm."

"But they would have harmed someone?" Bainbridge suggested. "Even if Underwood won his matches fairly, some would take affront at the fact he had bet upon himself and might think he had fixed the bout."

"Simon would never fix a fight!" Ottoman said with fiery pride at his late friend's integrity. "That was why he always bet on himself to win. There is nothing wrong with that, not really. He wasn't changing the outcome of the match."

"So you say, Mr Ottoman, but my point is that someone might have taken against him for making a little extra on the side," Bainbridge replied.

Ottoman was shaking his head.

"No, it wasn't like that."

"How was it you arrived here just as we did?" Victoria asked him.

The change of direction threw Ottoman for a second. He rallied magnificently.

"Coincidence, that is all."

"I suspect Mr Ottoman started to think about those unclaimed betting slips after we had paid him a visit," Bainbridge said to Victoria. "He suddenly recalled them and decided that if the police had not taken them, then he ought to. No doubt he had to wait for an opportune moment to leave his shop, which happened to coincide with us coming here."

"See?" Ottoman pointed at Bainbridge. "Coincidence! He said it."

"Since you have already indicated you refuse to be helpful to us, I think it is time we left and you must leave these rooms too, Mr Ottoman," Bainbridge said coldly.

"Now, wait a second," Ottoman raised a hand. "You can't just walk off with those betting slips."

"We can," Victoria promised him.

Ottoman had a weaselly, pathetic look on his face. He gulped.

"You see, here is the thing at the heart of it all. My shop is on hard times and I had to borrow some money. Those betting slips would cover my repayments."

"I am assuming that you did not borrow this money from a bank?" Bainbridge said to him in a voice that suggested he was both disappointed but not surprised.

Ottoman had broken out into a sweat.

"You are not wrong about that. I borrowed from some bad people. I know it was a silly thing to do, but I was desperate. Simon said he was going to help me out, give me some money from betting on himself. He had a big match coming up and he was going to earn a lot from the bets he had placed."

"That would be the match between him and Duncan Head," Bainbridge nodded. "We have seen the posters."

"It was going to be Simon's breakthrough, after that he was going to go professional. There would be lots of money. No more cheap attic rooms. No more street fights," Ottoman said this with a glimmer in his eyes. Those had been good dreams. "I thought to myself, seeing as he is dead and cannot mind, and seeing as he had already mentioned about giving me the money, it would do no harm to claim those betting slips."

Bainbridge had become distracted from the man's saga of woe and had turned his attention to one of the magazines on the table which had an article concerning Simon Underwood's forthcoming fight.

"How did Mr Underwood manage to secure a legitimate boxing match?" he asked Ottoman.

"People saw him, thought he was good," Ottoman said

coyly.

"You need the right people to see you," Bainbridge pointed out. "People like that are not necessarily hanging around street fights."

"Some do," Ottoman said sheepishly.

"Underwood was, what, forty years old?"

"Thirty-seven," Ottoman corrected him.

"Thirty-seven. That is rather old to begin a career as a professional boxer. All these boxers in these magazines, they are in their twenties and began their careers a good deal younger than that. Underwood was late to the scene."

"If you mean he was incapable of boxing for real…" Ottoman snapped.

"I meant," Bainbridge interrupted him. "It is remarkable that a boxing scout would show interest in a man of his age, purely because they are looking for young talent with many years ahead of them."

"Simon was as fit as a flea and had donkeys' years left in him," Ottoman responded brightly.

"Except he was not," Victoria carefully pointed out. "He was suffering from what I believe is termed a grumbling appendix. The blow to his belly ruptured it, but it would have done that itself sooner rather than later."

Ottoman looked at her aghast.

"What?"

"You do realise that your friend was living on borrowed time. Without medical treatment to remove his appendix, he was doomed," Victoria explained.

"Simon was as fit as a flea," Ottoman repeated, though just a hint of uncertainty had entered his voice.

"That is beside the point," Bainbridge interjected. "What we are really concerned about is how this boxing match was setup and who would or would not benefit from it?"

"I do not see how that is important?" Ottoman had been flummoxed by the news his friend had been dying and was now trying to catch up with the conversation.

"It possibly is not," Bainbridge admitted. "But since no

one is offering us an explanation for who wished Simon Underwood harm, and who attacked him that night..."

Ottoman started to speak, and Bainbridge held up a finger to stop him.

"Let us not repeat the nonsense concerning Franklin Ward, we both know he was not responsible though he did have reason to dislike Simon."

"Which, by the way was very mean," Victoria rounded on Ottoman. "Poor Franklin, why did Mr Underwood attack him like that?"

"It was just what Simon did," Ottoman shrugged. "He liked a fight."

"And you found that acceptable, did you?" Victoria demanded.

Ottoman looked cowed.

"I didn't say I liked it, but Simon was a good friend."

"And it was better to be on his side than against him," Bainbridge concluded.

"Franklin brought it on himself. He made a fuss in the pub, and that stirred Simon up. If he had said nothing, we would not be here."

"If Franklin had died because of the injuries he sustained at the hands of Mr Underwood, would you be so quick to defend your friend?" Victoria asked him.

Ottoman gaped at her, as if the question were self-explanatory.

"Simon never killed anyone."

"Yet, if he had, he would be the one in police custody. Even if Franklin did punch him back, which he did not and certainly not in the way your original story stated, well, it was no different to Underwood attacking him outside the pub. Underwood was, in fact, worse, for Franklin had not thrown a blow at him. You have double standards Mr Ottoman. If Franklin brought Underwood's wrath upon himself, then surely the same could be said in reverse?" Victoria concluded.

"I don't..." Ottoman scratched his head. "That is not the same."

"Yes, I see that," Victoria sighed. "Hence the problem we are having."

Ottoman was confused. She was saying things that made him doubt himself, doubt his friend Simon and that was unthinkable. Simon had always been good to him and he never meant any real harm when he started a fight. No one had ever died. He wasn't a bad person, but people were trying to make out he was, and Ottoman was getting muddled by it all.

"Back to the matter of the boxing match," Bainbridge said. "As no one has offered us a proper explanation for what happened to Underwood, it is necessary for us to explore every conceivable avenue of his life that might offer a solution, including his new career as a boxer."

Bainbridge had picked up the magazine and folded the pages back to present the article that interested him.

"Interesting odds," Bainbridge said. "I would think it unusual that the newcomer to a match should have better odds than his opponent who is recognised in the sport."

"Yeah, but Head is coming back from injury," Ottoman said, at last on a subject he was knowledgeable about. "He didn't win a single bout last year before he hurt his eye. Some say the eye injury was a sham to get him some time out of the sport. Putting Simon against him was a good entry into professional boxing for him. It was going to be an easy win to gain Simon some publicity."

"Then why was Head fighting him?" Victoria asked. "If everyone was so sure he would lose?"

"There is always a chance, and when you are a man who makes a living fighting, you take chances," Bainbridge explained. "I should imagine Head is tied into a contract too, has to compete in so many fights under its terms."

"How awful," Victoria said.

"Simon was not going to be contracted to anyone," Ottoman said proudly. "I heard him say that in this very room. 'I won't be contracted to anyone,' he said."

"A fine sentiment, but not how the sport works," Bainbridge put down the magazine. "Well, as you have proven yourself yet again to be a dead end, we are done here Mr Ottoman."

"But the slips!" Ottoman protested.

"I have already explained that they are evidence for the police and that is final," Bainbridge informed him fiercely. "You are to leave, at once."

Protesting, Ottoman was shooed out of the sitting room and into the tight little corridor.

"This is not what Simon intended," he said miserably. "He meant for me to have the money, he did!"

"Mr Ottoman, your financial problems, while sad, are none of my concern, and I cannot give you these slips until the case is resolved," Bainbridge waved at him like he was a fluttering chicken loose in the yard.

Ottoman, with the alert ears of someone who is always looking for a way out of trouble, had caught hold of what Bainbridge had said.

"Did you say when this case was finished I could have the slips?" he asked.

"Possibly," Bainbridge said, which actually meant 'not at all,' but he had not become a detective by failing to see when an opportunity was arising.

Ottoman had one foot out of the door.

"If someone was to assist in having this case resolved, you would be able to give up those slips sooner, yes?" Ottoman asked.

"Potentially," Bainbridge said. "Why, are you wishing to offer your help?"

Ottoman looked like he was about to spit something out, a secret he was rather desperate to tell. But the draw of the betting slips was not as strong as whatever it was that was holding him back and he slammed his mouth shut and shook his head.

"Never mind," he said, turning around sharply and rushing downstairs.

Bainbridge sighed.

"So close," he locked the door to Underwood's rooms.

"He might come around once he has time to consider,"

Victoria suggested.

"He might," Bainbridge did not hold out hope. "In the meantime, I wish to speak to the gentleman who is in charge of organising Duncan Head's boxing matches."

"Who is that?" Victoria asked.

"Charlie Trenchard," Bainbridge replied. "I read the name in the magazine. He had some history with Houston."

"Did he?"

"Yes, another case years ago if memory serves me. We shall go home first and I shall search my archives for details."

He started down the stairs.

"Did Houston often follow cases without you?" Victoria asked, walking behind him slowly. Bainbridge did not go down a set of stairs any faster than he went up them.

"Occasionally, but he always told me about them," Bainbridge replied.

"Hm," said Victoria.

Bainbridge did not like what that noise implied.

Chapter Sixteen

An introduction to Bainbridge's archival system was an education unto itself, or so Houston had once said. There was a library within Bainbridge's home, and it contained every case the pair had been involved in either individually or together. Houston had never had an issue placing the details of his personal cases within the archives, or so he had always said. Recent events had made Bainbridge begin to wonder if his late friend really had been so generous with his work, or whether he had been holding something back, and if so, what?

Bainbridge was endeavouring to shake off such thoughts as he showed Victoria the vast library. It was quite literally the biggest room in the house, having been created by the merging of two upper rooms. It did not just contain files on every case Bainbridge and Houston had investigated, but a large collection of newspaper clippings both English and American, and a diverse range of books on every subject under the sun that could be relevant to crime, including a few that Victoria could not fathom the purpose of. How did the Beginners Guide to Chinese

Porcelain have any value in a detective's library? Or The Folklore and Meaning of Flowers? Victoria felt impolite asking about them bluntly, especially as she felt being allowed into Bainbridge's library was a significant moment, a sign, if you will, that she had been accepted as a fellow detective at last.

She wondered if it was possible to ever understand the intricate and complex way Bainbridge filed everything in the place, or whether that was a secret science unique to her uncle's beautifully bent mind.

"Case files on the left. Bookcases labelled I to XXXII," Bainbridge pointed out the Roman numerals upon each tall bookcase. "Categorised by name of victim, name of client, name of suspect, name of perpetrator (if different to the suspect), date, month, location and whether it was a joint or single operation by either myself or Houston."

Victoria looked at the files, each housed in uniform brown cardboard folders with long numbers listed down the edges.

"Well," she said, wondering how on earth she was supposed to extrapolate a particular case from these anonymous rows of numbers. "that is certainly… thorough."

"There is a card catalogue, naturally," Bainbridge strolled over to a wooden filing case with very small drawers. When he pulled out a drawer it proved to be just big enough to house a rectangle of card. These cards were arranged in long rows numbering, Victoria could only guess, in the thousands. "The cards are alphabetical. Here, this one comes under T and we find the name Trenchard listed. It has a cross-reference to other cards that might warrant our attention and also lists the specific file we should find details about that case in."

"This is very admirable. It must take many hours to keep updated," Victoria frowned, having a terrible vision of herself spending lengthy afternoons writing up endless cards in this fashion.

"I do it all myself. Houston never mastered the system.

He would miss information out. Just lately I have added a few new categories to aid us, including type of crime, weapon used if relevant, motive, whether the perpetrator is a repeat offender and the gender of both victim and offender."

"Oh," Victoria said, unable to think of anything better.

"I also have listings for cases that are closed and that are open. Occasionally, both myself and Houston would take an interest in an older case that had never been solved by the police and would begin investigating it in our spare time. All files related to such cases and any ongoing ones, are kept in that bookcase."

Bainbridge pointed to bookcase XXXIII, which was one of the few with empty spaces. That, at least, was positive, indicating that this intensive over-filing had some benefit to solving crime.

"And you will file this case we are currently working on with this system?"

"Of course, though I have not had a chance to write much down as yet. That will come afterwards, when we are considering everything and putting together evidence for the police."

Bainbridge was taking note of the number listed under the word 'Trenchard'. Victoria glanced over his shoulder and glanced at the date of the case. 1888.

"This is an old case," she said.

"Old is relative," Bainbridge countered. "Memories of grievances and hurts are some of the most eternal we possess."

He walked over to bookcase XXV and started to run a finger along the spines of the many files. Bending each gently back so he could read it easier. Victoria cast her eyes around the expansive room while he searched, thinking that should she desire to, it would be simply impossible to read each and every book within these walls in a lifetime. She had been in libraries before, of course, the public sort and a few in the homes of her parents' friends, but never had she seen anything quite like this in a person's home.

She was a touch overwhelmed by the sheer weight of literature bearing down on her as she stood in one spot. It was intimidating in a bizarre way.

"Ah, here we go!" Bainbridge pulled a file off a shelf and wandered over to a long table with comfortable green leather seats either side. He settled himself into a chair with his customary groan.

Victoria took a seat beside him.

"Charlie Trenchard," Bainbridge read out the title. "If memory serves me, he was involved in a betting scandal which Houston unravelled. He ended up spending several years in prison."

"And now he runs legal boxing matches?" Victoria said, hoping she had laced that statement with enough cynical scepticism to draw Bainbridge's approval.

Her uncle smiled at her.

"The world is forever going about in circles," Bainbridge nodded. "Still, in the scheme of things, cheating people out of money they willingly risked is not quite so troubling as, say, murdering old ladies in their beds. I suppose the police find it more prudent to put their resources elsewhere."

Bainbridge started taking papers from the file. There was a photograph which he offered to Victoria.

"Mr Trenchard?" she asked.

"Yes. Houston was hired to investigate Trenchard by a group of gentlemen who suspected match fixing was occurring. He did not have to dig deep to unearth the truth."

Bainbridge laid out betting slips and tally sheets upon the table. There were handwritten notes in a script that Victoria did not recognised. It took her just a second to realise this was the handwriting of Houston Fairchild. The large, looping letters, the words spaced out across the paper as if they had had an argument, the occasional flourish on the end of a word, all reminded her of the larger than life American who she had never really had the chance to get to know. Her mother had always kept her away, feeling Houston was a bad influence (he had, in fairness to her mother, been known to swear before Victoria as a child, which was probably why she was drawn to him) and she had always intended, one day, when she was suitably grown and no longer under her mother's dictatorship, to get to know him properly. There had always seemed plenty of time for such a thing, and then Houston was gone.

Bainbridge had paused over the papers, feeling the influence of the man who had written them just as she did. His hand was trembling a little. Instinctively, Victoria reached out and clasped his hand in hers. Her uncle looked up at her with the saddest eyes and she felt his pain in that moment. She wished they had not come here, had not found this file, and started to read it.

"I could put it back," she said, starting to gather up the papers.

"No," Bainbridge said, his voice choked. "I cannot hide away from this forever, and we have a case to solve."

He started to go through the papers again.

"Aha, yes, I was sure I kept a clipping concerning Trenchard's incarceration. He was sentenced to ten years in Norwich prison," Bainbridge held out a newspaper clipping.

"He hasn't been out very long," Victoria worked out the dates in her mind. "He has been out, what, six months?"

"Around that," Bainbridge concurred. "Something does not sit right with all this. A man does not step out of prison and walk right back into the career that caused him to be incarcerated in the first place. Not after ten years."

"From the information we have gathered, it appears that Trenchard is operating as a respectable and legitimate boxing match organiser. At least on the surface."

"Someone has helped him out," Bainbridge mused. "I wonder who his contacts were before he went to prison?"

He rifled through the papers, looking for more information and pulled out a list of names entitled 'Known Associates'. Bainbridge ran a finger down the list.

"Well, well."

"Well, well?" Victoria repeated.

"I should not be unduly surprised. Upon this list is the name of Mr James Black, otherwise known as Jimmy Black."

Bainbridge pointed out the name to her.

"The man Underwood saw in The Toby Jug that night and decided it would be best to avoid," Victoria said. "Who is this man everyone seems worried about?"

"In the scheme of things, he is not anyone at all," Bainbridge explained. "You would not find his name known beyond the confines of this city. Most of those inhabitants of Norwich who walk in middle- and upper-class circles will never have heard his name. Even among those in the working classes, if they live respectably and keep out of trouble, they probably will not recognise the name, or will have only heard it in passing. However, within the world of crime and dark deeds, Black is a name that makes a person tremble.

"He is an organiser. I can think of no better way to put it. He has a finger in every pie available. If it is criminal, of course. He made his success because he is very clever and good with names and numbers. He sees opportunities others do not. You see, what holds back most criminals, what, it could be argued, thrusts them into crime in the first place, is a lack of a solid education. I do not call them stupid, though some are, but stupidity does not make a man naturally inclined to do wrong. No, I am talking about men and women who, through circumstances outside their control, have never had the chance to improve themselves and benefit from an education.

"They stumble into crime as it seems the only way forward for them. But Mr Black, he is another class of criminal altogether. He is intelligent and well educated. He has the sort of mind that can run figures together in seconds and see the potential in them. That was how he found his niche. He proposed himself as the mind behind the crime. Helped other established criminals to make bigger profits with less risk and slowly worked his way up."

"He sounds quite the entrepreneur," Victoria said. "But why is everyone so afraid of him?"

Bainbridge had a strange smile on his face.

"The world Black runs in is not one where you can exist for long without collecting enemies. Black swiftly realised that to survive in this new world, to profit from it, he must gather around him men who would protect him. They must also enforce his will. When someone does not pay him his share from a crime, for instance, so he must make them examples to others who would see him as weak, someone they could use. Black now has a gang of enforcers and bodyguards who are the thugs behind his brains. It is not so much Black people fear, as the goons he controls. Not to mention that Black can call in a favour from near enough anyone within the Norfolk criminal world if he wishes to. You do not tread on Black's toes without good reason, and good protection."

"I suppose, then, it is not really surprising Black's name would feature on a list of associates of Trenchard?" Victoria said thoughtfully.

"Yes, and no," Bainbridge replied. "Houston would not have listed the name unless he was aware there was a solid connection between them. By that I mean that Trenchard was either working for, or with, Black. Yet Black's name never came up in the trial. The police have been trying to nail some crime to him for years."

"Why was Underwood worried about him?" Victoria said aloud.

"Well, first things first, no one disturbs Jimmy Black when he is having a quiet drink."

"That is a rule, is it?"

"A firm rule," Bainbridge nodded. "Underwood saw Black sitting there and had the sense to think twice about starting a fight."

"Well, then, we must speak to Trenchard and determine what he knows," Victoria said, feeling better about the idea now. "It seems curious that a man like him, would have found himself a respectable trade in boxing matches. This Duncan Head, for instance, is a celebrity boxer, yes?"

"Yes, and if you are meaning why would he get himself involved with a man like Trenchard, well, I find that curious too. He should have his own agent, one he has been with years," Bainbridge scratched his chin. "I do not have any sporting magazines within my collections. How remiss of me. If I did, we might have been able to peruse them for details on Head's sporting career."

"I suppose we shall just have to do things the old-fashioned way," Victoria smiled to herself.

"What way is that?" Bainbridge asked.

"We must ask him," Victoria responded.

"Ah, that old-fashioned way," Bainbridge grunted, rising from his chair to replace the file. "I thought you meant something else."

"Such as?"

Bainbridge hesitated.

"In a flash of quite random thought, I found myself thinking of the Spanish Inquisition and, quite remarkably, the term 'thumb screws' jumped into my mind, when you mentioned 'old-fashioned methods'. I fear my brain turns in strange ways."

Victoria looked at him aghast.

"Yes," Bainbridge said, clearing his throat. "I thought that might be your response. Still, it was just a thought. No harm ever came from thoughts."

Bainbridge purposefully walked towards the bookcase to restore the case file.

"Thumb screws?" Victoria called out behind him.

He turned on his heel and looked at her sheepishly.

"You thought I was suggesting we should rough someone up for information?" Victoria persisted.

"I did think it was somewhat unusual for you," Bainbridge replied. "But one can never quite tell."

Victoria glared at him. Bainbridge made a great act of putting away the case file. Victoria shook her head.

"I do not know what to say!"

"My dear Vicky, when it comes to it, I could have thought a lot worse," Bainbridge told her, endeavouring to cheer her up.

Victoria was mollified at first, then she ran his words through her mind.

"How much worse?"

Chapter Seventeen

Charlie Trenchard had not suffered as much as might be imagined from his time in prison. He lived in a nice little house towards the outskirts of town. Two up, two down, with a garden at the front and back. Victoria reflected that a life of crime, even if it were just swindling foolish men who could not resist a gamble, had paid off for Charlie. She was not impressed.

"How can he afford such a place after ten years in prison?" she said to Bainbridge.

"Indeed," Bainbridge looked at the house from his seat in the car. "I imagine the police never did discover where he had hidden his ill-gotten gains."

"He was very successful?" Victoria asked.

"Highly. It was why the case was significant."

Bainbridge descended from the car with the grace of a badger that has fallen off a log. There was a moment when he was suspended by the sheer determination of his arms and then he alighted to the ground and adjusted his shirt.

"They have not quite mastered car design yet, have they?" he said over his shoulder as Victoria dropped to the ground gracefully.

"Sorry?" she said.

"Never mind," Bainbridge answered.

They walked up to the house door, through a garden that had been recently and in a rather heavy-handed way, remodelled. Flowerbeds had been weeded to within an inch of their lives and several rose bushes were looking almost naked after a severe pruning. It was almost, Bainbridge thought to himself, as if someone were making up for ten years of neglect.

There was a bell hanging next to the door. Bainbridge rang it with a vigorous clatter.

"You are thinking Trenchard had money stashed away for a rainy day," Victoria said as the clanging drifted back into silence.

"I think a man does not come out of prison and straight into a fine house like this without a little help," Bainbridge said. "I also think money can buy respectability in certain circles."

Victoria considered this for a moment, then realised he was referring to Trenchard's leap back into boxing matches. Yes, money could have paved the way for that.

The door opened a fraction, and in the gap stood a man who could have been Charlie Trenchard, if you took into account the deterioration time and a prison sentence can cause. Trenchard had a haggard look to him, there were lines on his forehead and around his neck, his complexion which had looked quite flawless in the photograph Victoria had seen, was now blotchy and there was a nasty scar across one cheek. In short, it had been a harrowing decade for the man and his face told the story.

"Good afternoon Mr Trenchard," Bainbridge held out his hand to the man to shake. "We have come to pass on our condolences for the passing of Mr Underwood."

Trenchard looked at Bainbridge's hand uncertainly, then he reached out and shook it.

"Yeah? Well, it is inconvenient," he muttered.

"I was most disheartened to hear the news," Bainbridge

persisted. "Why, I went to buy tickets for the match between him and Duncan Head and was informed of the cancellation. What a shock."

"You have to roll with the punches," Trenchard shrugged. "To use a boxing term."

"And I was so looking forward to seeing Head back in action after his long recovery from injury," Bainbridge continued freely.

Trenchard tilted his head to one side.

"You had heard about that?" he said.

"Mr Head had been away from the boxing scene a while and, please excuse my bluntness, but the change of management on his part suggested some sort of difficult circumstance befalling him."

Victoria was watching her uncle, intrigued how he had wriggled out this piece of insight from the facts before him. It turned out he was perfectly correct.

"Yes, well, the eye injury took a long time to heal and his former management weren't prepared to wait," Trenchard sniffed. "You know how these folks are. It's all about the money, rather than the man."

Trenchard sounded quite indignant about his statement, which was ironic.

"It could have been the end of Mr Head's career," Bainbridge added. "How fortunate you came along, Mr Trenchard. Why, think what talent we would have lost from the world."

"Yeah," Trenchard said, preening a little under Bainbridge's praise. "Well, you know how it is."

He cleared his throat.

"Did you want something specific?"

"Oh my, did I forget to say?" Bainbridge acted as if he were a blustering old fool that would forget his own name if he wasn't careful. "I came to see if you might have had any signed pictures of Mr Underwood? I collect them, you see, and I was sure I would get one on the match night, but now of course… and they must be quite a rare thing."

"Rare?" Trenchard's ears perked up.

"Why yes, the picture of a fighter who never got to fight. I should think, given time, they ought to be worth some money. What you would call a collector's item, I imagine."

Trenchard's eyes had lit up. The key to him was money and any opportunity to make it. A slight smile graced his lips, then he remembered Bainbridge was there.

"Now, ahem, you want one of those pictures?"

"If they exist. I assume you had some made up to hand out to the crowd?"

"Of course, of course. Now, if I were to let you have one for a reasonable sum, perhaps you could spread the word about them? Let others know that they could be a... a.... what did you call them again?"

"A collector's item," Bainbridge beamed.

"That's it," Trenchard said happily. "Yes, can't have them going to waste now. Why don't you come in?"

He allowed them into his snug home, showing them into a sitting room with an array of prints on the walls depicting various boxing matches. In graceful script beneath the etched images were their titles. Here was the famous 1872 boxing match between Lord Selby and Black Bill, and here was another from 1880 illustrating the knockout blow given by Harry Burke to Edward Graceling. Bainbridge took a good look at the prints.

"You have had quite the illustrious career in boxing," he remarked to Trenchard. "I am surprised I have not heard your name before. I have been following the sport these last five or six years."

"I retired for a while," Trenchard said with barely a pause. "You know how it is, always on the go, never time for yourself. Finally, I needed a break."

"Of course," Bainbridge nodded. "I am correct to say there was a scandal revolving around the Burke/Graceling match, something to do with Graceling taking an early fall?"

"You must be thinking of another match," Trenchard said without hesitation. "I'll go get those pictures."

Trenchard left the room and Victoria glanced at her uncle.

"What are you doing?" she asked him.

Bainbridge gave her a puzzled look.

"Interrogating the man," he replied.

"Are you not going to ask him directly how he came to be arranging a boxing match when he has spent the last ten years in prison?"

"Do you imagine he will answer such a question?" Bainbridge asked her.

Victoria fell silent.

"Well, no."

"Then I shall quietly edge my way around the houses and see what I can wheedle out. Right in this moment, I do not want Trenchard to know we are detectives."

Victoria would have said more, but Trenchard was returning with the pictures he had promised.

"I could charge a pound for them, don't you think?" he said to Bainbridge.

He handed a photograph to the colonel. It showed Underwood in a standard boxing stance, fists raised, eyes centred on the camera. He looked big and menacing.

"I think you could," Bainbridge said, without offering any money himself. Trenchard looked crestfallen and about ready to take back the picture. "You know, I was quite surprised that a man of Underwood's age should just be starting his boxing career."

Trenchard's fingers were twitchy near the picture.

"Sorry, what?"

"I am surprised that at his age, anyone would be considering Underwood as a fighter," Bainbridge repeated himself. "He was considerably older than most budding boxers."

"He was no spring chicken..." Trenchard agreed reluctantly.

"Someone must have thought he was a worthwhile prospect, though," Bainbridge added, turning over the picture in his hand. "Ah, no details about him listed. I do like details. Of course, we have no fight records to put down, but I should be able to make up some sort of listing. Who was his manager?"

"Underwood rather managed himself," Trenchard replied.

Bainbridge had never heard such hokum before, well, actually he had, but not in the context of a boxing match.

"Someone must have proposed him to you," he insisted. "Unless you mean he simply turned up on your doorstep one day and asked to be given the chance to fight."

"No, of course not," Trenchard laughed. "I wouldn't have given him the time of day."

"Then, precisely how did he find his way to you?"

Trenchard was not looking happy about the direction the conversation was taking. He put a grin on his face, but it did not seem very friendly.

"Here, if you want that picture, I shall be needing a pound."

Bainbridge ignored this change of subject.

"I think someone suggested him as a soft target for Head's first match back, am I right?" he said instead.

Trenchard was uneasy. He wanted to grab the picture from Bainbridge's hand and shove his guests out of the front door, but the part of him that was keen for opportunity, would not allow him to give up any chance he might have of making more money.

"Head needs a sensible comeback match," Trenchard added. "Nothing too rigorous. Nothing with too much pressure."

"Underwood was a fearsome fighter," Bainbridge said. "I saw him in a street fight once."

Trenchard was intrigued by this news. He had not considered Bainbridge the sort to watch a street fight.

"You did?"

"I sometimes indulge in these things," Bainbridge hedged. "Underwood was not an easy target."

"Head needed a decent opponent," Trenchard sniffed. "Someone on the up, who would appreciate the situation."

"Yes, that is what I thought," Bainbridge said darkly. "Quite lucky you came across Underwood."

"It was, but I shall find another," Trenchard was anxious again. "Did you want that picture."

Bainbridge glanced over the image in his hand.

"I think perhaps not, if you are asking a pound."

He started to hand it back.

"Two shillings, then?"

"Had the match gone ahead, these would have been handed out for free," Bainbridge reminded him.

"But it didn't," Trenchard said, annoyed at the loss of a sale. He grabbed back the picture. "Time for you to be going."

He was motioning towards the hallway and the front door.

"Are you aware that the police are treating Underwood's death as a murder?" Bainbridge asked, not moving.

"I heard something," Trenchard said, annoyed he could not get rid of his guests.

"They might be very interested to learn that Charlie Trenchard was in charge of a fight Underwood should have been in," Bainbridge pressed.

Trenchard had been half-listening, now his full attention was upon them. He gulped, but his eyes sparkled dangerously.

"What did you say?"

"I know who you are Charlie Trenchard," Bainbridge said. "I know where you have been these last ten years and why your garden was overgrown, and you had not been heard of in so long."

"I don't think you know anything," Trenchard snapped.

"I know you were in prison for match fixing," Bainbridge explained. "I know there was something fishy about the match between Underwood and Head."

"I would like you to leave now," Trenchard said, no more humour in his voice. He walked firmly to his front door and opened it for them.

"Head needs a comeback match, and Underwood was supplied as his opponent, yet he was clearly a strong fighter, not an easy choice," Bainbridge persisted. "Unless, of course, some arrangement had been come to before then."

Trenchard scowled at him.

"I want you to leave!"

"Fine, fine," Bainbridge smiled at him. "But, before I go, perhaps you would care to tell me how Underwood came to your attention."

"No, I would not care!" Trenchard snapped. "You are not really boxing enthusiasts, are you?"

Bainbridge gave a little apologetic bow.

"You are correct on that front. I am a good friend of Franklin Ward."

"Who?" Trenchard snarled, confused.

"The man who has been falsely accused of murdering Mr Underwood. It is quite apparent to anyone who cares to pay attention to the facts that Underwood was targeted deliberately due to some grudge, not at all as his friends have described his accident. I have no real interest in your business Mr Trenchard, if you care to fix matches there are others who can take grievance at that, not I. My interest is purely in finding the real culprit behind the death of Simon Underwood so Franklin will be set free."

"I don't know anything about any of this," Trenchard said moodily. "I am out of pocket, you know, because of the failure of this match!"

"Then it would be in your interest to find who did this too," Victoria pointed out.

Trenchard was not impressed.

"Hardly makes any difference to me!" he spluttered. "Now, clear off! I have a match to reschedule."

"Of course," Bainbridge gave him a polite smile as if they were just having a pleasant tete-a-tete. "By the way, Houston Fairchild sends his best wishes."

The colour drained from Trenchard's face.

"Clear off!" he yelled.

They had done what they could and now they left the house, retreating to Victoria's car.

"Why did you say that about Houston?" Victoria asked her uncle.

"I wanted to see his reaction. You notice he seemed alarmed at the name but did not appear to be aware that Houston is dead?"

"You thought he might have had something to do with that?"

"Not really," Bainbridge shrugged. "I rather wanted to rattle him for my own amusement and you never know what might come from it. In any case, it is interesting to learn that in certain quarters Houston's death has yet to be reported."

Victoria placed her hands on the steering wheel.

"Where to now?" she asked.

"Oh, I think our next port of call must be Mr Head, who may reveal more than his so-called management. In particular, I want to know how he has ended up associated with Trenchard."

"That was a good guess about him being injured," Victoria complimented him.

"It was based on the facts before me. But yes, a guess. Now, if I have this correct, we need to go to the end of the road and turn left."

"How did you get Head's address?" Victoria asked.

Bainbridge gave her an aghast look.

"My dear, I am a detective!"

Chapter Eighteen

The weather had turned as they trundled along. There was a hint of rain in the air. Bainbridge was thinking he ought to have brought an umbrella, the barometer had indicated a change in pressure that morning. Mrs Huggins had complained about her knees, and that reminded him that she always complained of her knees when it was going to rain. Moodily, Bainbridge contemplated the possibility of getting wet.

"As much as I am enjoying your car, Vicky, I find it inconvenient that it does not have a roof," he said when a fat raindrop landed squarely on his nose with the assurance that there were more to follow.

"Oh, it has a roof!" Victoria said brightly. "I just have no idea how to raise it up."

"Possibly now would be the time to investigate the matter?" Bainbridge suggested as the errant raindrop's comrades joined the fray.

Victoria pulled the car to a halt and looked over her shoulder behind the seats were Bainbridge could now see a pile of folded leather. Victoria pulled at it tentatively and it unfurled as if attached to some sort of leverage system.

"Oh, it seems quite straightforward," she said optimistically. Then she pulled harder at the leather and it unfolded in a graceful arch, revealing that it had a framework of brass struts holding it in place.

Victoria pulled it as far out as it would go and then released it, whereupon the leather started to slowly fold back on itself. Bainbridge was just getting settled beneath the new roof and was alarmed at this predicament.

"It must have to attach to something," he declared, grabbing frantically at a strut to prevent himself from being exposed to the rain.

Victoria stood thoughtfully studying the car for some time and then reached a conclusion.

"It probably attaches here, to the upright of the windscreen," she said. "There even appears to be a catch for it."

She pulled the roof forward once more and with a cry of triumph secured it to the upright. Bainbridge was able to do the same to his side. They succeeded just in time, for the clouds had burst and a summer shower was hammering down upon them. Victoria hastened back into the car.

"It does not leak at all," she said, feeling the roof above her.

There was one downside to being safely installed in the car while it rained outside. No one had supplied the vehicle with a means for clearing rain from the windscreen, so at points along the rest of their journey, Victoria was unable to see where she was going. They took things even slower than usual.

Mr Head had lodgings in a boarding house. In Bainbridge's expert opinion of boarding houses (for he had come across quite a few in his time) this one fell into the category of being largely respectable. There were notices in the window that advised those entering the premises that there was no drinking, no smoking, and no swearing beyond the threshold of the door. There was no directive concerning the oldest vice in the world, but Bainbridge was confident that was banned too. Despite the strictures imposed on tenants, or possibly because of them, the house proudly indicated on another sign that it had no vacancies.

They descended from the car and entered via a recently painted green door, finding themselves in a modest reception area, with a table and a bell. Yet another handwritten noticed encouraged them to ring the bell for service.

Before he could stop her, this was exactly what Victoria did.

"There was no rush," Bainbridge hissed at her.

"Why should I not ring the bell, the sign told me to do so."

"I was getting a feel for the place," Bainbridge huffed, his professional pride dented. He should have been the one to ring the bell and take the lead.

Victoria made that snorting noise which he was learning implied she was less than impressed by his response. It was making Bainbridge self-conscious.

"Yes?" a woman with a spidery appearance and wearing a good deal of black lace (the cheap sort, made on machines and not as pretty as the hand-woven stuff) appeared through a doorway. She was looking down her nose at them, even though they were probably the most respectable people who had ever walked through her door.

"Good afternoon, madam," Bainbridge removed his hat and was at his most obsequious. "We are looking for Mr Edward Head, if he is about?"

The woman gave him an assessing look. She did not appear to like what she saw.

"Who are you?"

"Colonel Bainbridge, and this is my niece," Bainbridge answered. "We hoped to speak to Mr Head about his boxing. We were most upset to learn his impending return match had been cancelled."

The landlady pricked up her ears.

"Cancelled?"

"Yes. Quite terrible. It must be a worry to the poor man

how to make ends meet, but the good news is we may have a solution for him."

Victoria gave him a sideways look of disapproval as he spun these lies, but Bainbridge was not ashamed to bend the truth when it got him what he needed. He had recognised a creature driven by money and the earning of the same in the landlady, and he was going to use that to his advantage.

The spidery woman was thinking hard, joining a few dots in her mind. Wondering if her tenant, Mr Head, was going to be able to afford this week's rent. She had plans for that rent, she had been saving up for some more lace, to finish off her widow's weeds. She did not want to have to wait any longer. Finally, she looked up at Bainbridge.

"Room three, it's up the stairs and on the left. It has a good outlook over the street," she said this with a hint of pride. "I should say I would not normally allow a woman in my rooms."

"However, she is my niece," Bainbridge suddenly seemed to have developed a hunch in his back and a tremble to his hand. "And I fear I shall never master those stairs alone."

Bainbridge placed a hand on the table and leaned down on it hard.

"Now Uncle," Victoria swept into action, understanding the charade, "we must have you sitting down at once. You know you should not be stood up for so long."

"I know, I know, but it was so very important I saw Mr Head and offered him my proposal," Bainbridge said, even his voice sounding weak now. He also loaded the word 'proposal', hoping to imply he was going to make a very good business deal to the man.

The landlady was following this with interest, she now saw there was a risk of the matter falling apart if she was obstructive any further, and she was very curious about the business proposal Bainbridge had hinted at.

"We cannot have you falling down, sir," she said, suddenly all good manners and no haughtiness. She took hold of Bainbridge's nearest arm. "I shall help escort you upstairs personally."

Victoria had Bainbridge's other arm.

"His knees are not what they were," she remarked to the landlady over her uncle's head.

"That was how my late Albert went, first his knees, then his heart," the landlady tutted to herself.

"I had not realised the two could be connected," Victoria said.

"Oh yes. Knees are the death of many folk," the landlady said sagely.

Bainbridge cast Victoria a worried look, suddenly concerned for his imminent doom. Then he reminded himself he didn't really have bad knees; he was just pretending. Sometimes he got carried away with himself...

The landlady deposited them before room three.

"Anything you need, I am just downstairs," she informed them with sudden kind generosity.

She gave Bainbridge a consoling pat on the shoulder, the sort you might give an old horse you were about to send to the knacker's yard and left them. Bainbridge stopped leaning against Victoria once she was gone.

"Thank goodness for that," Victoria groaned. "You are heavy!"

"It is all my muscle," Bainbridge replied sniffily.

"I would like to know what muscle that is," Victoria pointed to his stomach.

Bainbridge clasped his hands around it as if he had been caught exposed.

"My dear, I am in fine physical form!"

"Yes, but for what species?" Victoria raised an eyebrow, then she knocked on the door of room three before he could reply.

"What?" someone called from within.

"He sounds drunk," Victoria hissed to Bainbridge. "Which is impossible, considering the notices in the windows."

Bainbridge wondered if it was worth pointing out that

a handwritten note glued to a windowpane was not, in itself, much use for preventing a determined soul bringing drink up to their room. He decided he did not have the energy.

"Mr Duncan Head? Might we have a moment of your time?" he called through the door instead.

There was movement within the room, and something fell over. Someone cursed to themselves.

"Potentially two notices ignored," Bainbridge muttered to himself.

Victoria looked at him sharply but had no time to ask what he meant as the door was then swung open and a bleary-eyed Duncan Head looked out at them.

He was wearing only trousers and a vest, his feet being bare and his hair uncombed. He ran fingers through it, causing it to spike up on end.

"Do I know you?" he asked them.

"Bainbridge Boxing Consortium," Victoria said before her uncle could begin. "We are an independent organisation looking to the welfare of boxers, current and retired. We believe the business is full of exploitation and wish to see our clients being treated fairly. We are a philanthropic institute and do not require you to pay us a penny."

Head gaped as she relayed this information. Bainbridge was not far behind him.

"Oh," Head rubbed at his face. "Well, look... best you come in."

He turned around and slumped into his room. With his back turned Victoria gave a smile to Bainbridge, proud of her subterfuge.

"Two can lie," she whispered as she followed the boxer.

Duncan rented a single room from his landlady. She had not been lying when she had said it had the best view in the house, indeed, it was probably the best room all told. A large bay window looked down into the street and provided plenty of light to the space. Like all such rooms, furniture was minimal. A bed against a wall served as a sofa as well, a narrow wardrobe up a corner offered storage. A small table with a single chair completed the fittings, and of course there was a fireplace. Head had cluttered up the space amid his furniture with discarded papers, clothing, and wrappers from food items. Bainbridge noticed a paper sheath from a bar of Caley's chocolate dotting the rug. There were quite a lot of sweet things, or at least the evidence for them, scattered on the floor. Head clearly had a sweet tooth. Paper sweet bags were all over the place, and a bag of humbugs was sitting half consumed on the table.

Head wandered over to his bed and slumped down, leaning forward so his hands hung between his knees. Victoria glanced at Bainbridge, at a loss what to say or do next.

"Mr Head," Bainbridge opened. "We have heard about your disappointment concerning your forthcoming match with Mr Underwood."

"Yeah, that was a disaster," Head rubbed a hand over his face. "That was my comeback match."

"We are aware," Bainbridge nodded. "Times have been difficult lately?"

Head shrugged.

"I took a bad blow to the eye a while ago. Doctors thought I might lose the vision in that eye," Head rubbed at his left eye socket thoughtfully. "They said the bone of the socket was likely crushed. Anyway, I got lucky and it healed but my vision is not as good as before. I can see plain as day, but sometimes I don't see blows coming at me. It's my reactions that have suffered. And I get these bad headaches."

"We disturbed you during one of these episodes?" Bainbridge observed.

Head repeated the shrug.

"I took some laudanum to try to sleep off the aches. I get these real cravings for sweet things too, I suppose that is linked to it," Head sighed. "I am not much of a boxer these days."

"The match with Underwood was to be your first fight

since your injury?" Victoria clarified.

"Yes," Head nodded, regretting the move at once. "It was going to be a fresh start. I have been training hard, getting my eye back in. I ain't perfect, but I can still throw a good punch."

There was a thread of pride still lingering within Head as he said this.

"May I ask, when did you come under the management of Mr Trenchard?" Bainbridge asked carefully, they were treading on treacherous ground now.

Head gave a weak smile.

"My old manager gave me up a couple of months after the eye injury. He was not convinced I could recover. I was useless to him. Younger men were waiting in the wings. I was old and probably finished," Head snorted. "I will show him."

"This is exactly what the consortium is concerned about, the exploitation of boxers who are then abandoned when something occurs to end or stall their career," Victoria said fiercely.

She was rather getting into her role.

Head tilted his chin and gave her such a sad, cynical expression she felt quite despondent.

"It is the way of the world," he said.

"It does not have to be…" Victoria began.

Bainbridge gently touched her arm. She had forgotten why they were really there, getting caught up in Head's story of plight.

"I must ask again, when you became a fighter for Mr Trenchard?" he said.

Head looked up at him, with eyes that looked red and sore.

"You know he is a crook, right?" the boxer asked.

"I am aware of his past," Bainbridge agreed.

"Well, he is the only one willing to take me on these days," Head replied. "About a month ago he approached me with the idea I box for him. I had been putting the word out I was ready to fight, to get back in the ring. My name got through to Trenchard."

Head laughed bitterly to himself.

"Who am I kidding? He was the only one interested in taking me on. I have no delusions on the matter. He is using me to turn a profit. But what am I going to do about it?"

"You know the match against Underwood was fixed?" Bainbridge asked.

Head gave him a slow grin.

Chapter Nineteen

The tale was sordid but not unexpected. Head, the aging boxer, had hoped for one final triumph, to stand in the spotlight of glory and feel the adoration of those watching. He wanted to prove he was not finished, even if to do so required him to cheat.

He had been off the scene for too long. His manager had dropped him, convinced he was through as a boxer. Head had found himself looking at an uncertain future. He had never planned for the day he could not fight, somehow, he had never expected it to come. Money grew tight as his recuperation dragged out. Initially he relied on his friends to help him survive, but that was not feasible long term. He picked up what work he could find, where he could find it. It was usually the back breaking laborious sort. Loading and unloading cargo from trains or carts or lifting sacks of sand and concrete at building sites. It was all he was good for and the realisation made him more and more despondent.

The headaches didn't help. They could be crippling, and all the doctors could suggest was laudanum, which made him sleepy and wretched. Sometimes, even with the drug, he could not get relief from his headaches. In this sorry state, often not fully aware of the world, he bumbled along, a faded, forgotten sort of man.

His first street fight began as a brawl. Someone had recognised him in a pub and had made a comment about how he was washed-up. Head took a swing at him and proved he still had a solid right hook. The fight was ushered outside by the landlord and there in the street, rain tumbling down on him and soaking his clothes, Head demonstrated that he was still a damn good boxer. He didn't learn until afterwards that bets had been placed. One spectator who was kinder than the rest and possibly recognised the difficult situation Head was in, handed him some money, shook his hand, and said he was glad to see him back on his feet.

It took time for all this to sink in and for Head to realise not only what had happened, but what possibilities lay ahead. It was not like the world he was used to. Street fighting was a world away from the legitimate boxing ring, but when you had been cast out to starve, what else could you do?

He started to pick fights for money. People would pay him to take on a fighter they proposed. The reasons why other fighters came to him were diverse – some wanted just to brawl, some wanted to prove themselves against a real boxer, some had a disturbing desire to just take him on and win. And so, he fought, and he lost a lot, that was the bitterness of it. He felt as if he was punching at the right time, but it was as if there was a delay with every swing. Blows that should have landed missed. Unfortunately, the reverse was rarely true. He had lost his ability to dodge as well as hit.

He blamed the laudanum. He blamed his eye. He blamed the headaches. He blamed everything he could but that did not change a thing. He spent a lot of time lying dazed on the cobbles, staring up at the stairs and worried faces. Each new failure seemed to worsen his problems. His head was always ringing. Ultimately, he knew this was not a lifestyle he could sustain.

He had considered it a stroke of good luck when he opened his eyes from another knockout blow and saw the face of Charlie Trenchard staring down at him. It took him a moment to recognise his face, but he had seen Trenchard around on the circuit, back in the day. He thought he looked rather worn around the edges, but then he supposed he was not much better.

Trenchard helped him up and bought him a pint. That was when he laid out his proposal. Trenchard wanted to get back into boxing after his stint in prison. They skipped delicately over the fact that it was his less than legal involvement in the sport that had resulted in prison time in the first place. Ten years was a long time and Trenchard had lost most of his contacts. The fighters he had once had under his banner had either gone with someone else or retired. In short, he was facing the prospect of starting completely afresh, having to build himself up once again and he was not relishing the idea. Then he spotted Head.

Of course, he knew who Head was. He had been famous in the boxing circles of Norwich back in the day. Younger boxers would speak of the 'Head stance' and 'swinging like Head'. To speak his name was at one time to speak of emulating him and his glory. Trenchard stirred up a lot of memories during their conversation, good memories. Head had looked back to another time when he was special, important, when there seemed no end to the possibilities before him. He missed that time.

When Trenchard laid out his proposition, he had already set down the groundwork by stirring up the old boxer's sentimental side. The plan was simple enough. Trenchard would be Head's new manager and arrange some fights for him, low level at first, just to bring him back onto the scene. His opponents would be carefully chosen, and Head would have a string of successes. Enough to make it seem he was back on top of his game.

Then would come the special match. An unknown

street fighter would be put up against Head. He would look the part, big and mean, but with Head's new reputation for being unstoppable it was going to be obvious where people would place their money. It was to be a ten-round fight. First few rounds Head would be brutal. His opponent would take some heavy punishment and be on the ground quicker than you could say punch. This would up the odds in Head's favour further.

At this point, someone would lay a large bet on his opponent to win. The odds would look pretty poor, but some fool was always willing to take a chance. A couple more rounds would go to Head and things would look settled, and then would come the deciding round. The pair would spar off, Head would lay some good blows, but suddenly the newcomer would come back with a punch that no one had expected, and Head would be crashing down, knocked out cold – or so it would appear. The match would be over, the newcomer declared the winner, and some very lucky soul would have made a small fortune on that risky bet he had laid.

"And you were happy with that," Bainbridge concluded.

"Yeah," Head said. "Not exactly noble, but the money would be good. I would get a cut, as would the newcomer."

"After that? What was Trenchard's long game?" Bainbridge asked.

"He was going to have me train up younger boxers for him. His plan was to open his own training venue. I would be a draw for him, big name from the past. I would pass on my tips, run the place."

"Not a bad arrangement," Victoria said kindly, for the weary boxer looked so miserable.

"No," he agreed. "But it wasn't who I am. A teacher? I am not sure I could stand it."

Head winced and clutched at his temple. Bainbridge frowned.

"Are they getting worse, the headaches?"

"Yeah," Head sighed. "I'm never free of them. Sometimes it takes all my strength just to get up off the bed."

Bainbridge did not add anything, but the silence that fell after his question seemed telling to them all.

"Why have you told us all this?" Victoria asked. "Are you not afraid we shall stop Trenchard's scheme?"

Head shrugged.

"I don't know if I care," he said. "I am not sure that I have much fight left in me. If there was a way you could help me, give me a comfortable retirement, it would be greatly appreciated."

Victoria's face fell as she realised he was referring to her made-up charity. Bainbridge avoided looking at her, as he knew his expression would appear smug. She had not thought through her lies.

"You wanted to hear the truth and to know about exploitation of boxers and I am giving it to you," Head added, starting to be troubled by her silence. "Don't tell me I have made a mistake trusting you."

"Mr Head, you have not," Victoria assured him. "However, the organisation is not... that is to say..."

She took a breath before she could blurt out.

"We do not have any funds to assist you."

Head took this stoically.

"Sounds about right for my luck."

"We shall, however, not say anything concerning Trenchard, since to do so would place you in a difficult position, and that was not our intention," Victoria hastened to add.

"You don't have to explain," Head sighed. "Honest, you don't."

"Mr Head, this is possibly not a question you can answer, but how comfortable with the arrangement of the match fix was Mr Underwood?" Bainbridge asked.

Head shrugged his shoulders.

"I never asked him."

"He must have agreed with the arrangement?"

"My understanding was that he was going to make a profit out of the matter too, so he was happy with it. And

Trenchard was offering to take him on as a boxer afterwards."

"Hm," Bainbridge nodded. He felt they had come to another dead end. The rigged boxing match had seemed a promising lead. Perhaps Underwood had been having doubts about the whole thing and the assault on him was meant as a warning? Except it appeared he had been quite settled about the matter and was not at all affected by his conscience.

Bainbridge was disappointed.

"It seems to me, Mr Head, that you would upset a lot of people by taking a fall?" Victoria said.

"Nature of the beast," Head shrugged his shoulders again, then winced as his head pounded. "That is why Trenchard was staging the whole thing, to make it look legitimate. He had gotten cocky before he went to prison, was not so careful about making it seem as if a match had just gone bad for the favourite. People noticed."

"Surely people would remember his name?" Victoria added.

Head gave her a lopsided smile.

"You would be amazed at how people forget. No one ever pays attention to the manager, anyway. Not when they are busy looking at the named star," he proudly clutched a fist to his chest. "We were going to rock the world, now... now, I just don't know."

"I was thinking of those people still loyally following you," Victoria said softly. "Your supporters."

"They supported me if it suited them," Head sniffed. "They only saw money when they thought of me."

"Oh," Victoria said. "I am sorry."

"There was one, though," Head said thoughtfully, as if he had just remembered something. "He always came to my matches and cheered me on. I did appreciate him and, now you mention it, I would have felt bad taking a deliberate fall with him watching."

"Then perhaps it is just as well the match is not to go ahead?" Victoria suggested.

"My one loyal supporter. Through thick and thin," Head muttered to himself. "Though, considering he had a bob or two, he could have helped me out a bit more after my injury."

Head snorted.

"That's how these people are. They are all users. Jimmy Black was just the same."

Bainbridge was roused by the mention of a familiar name.

"Jimmy Black was your biggest supporter?"

"Through thick and thin," Head repeated solemnly. "I once boxed a match for his birthday. Glory days those were. Glory days."

Head sighed to himself, then he laid back on his bed and rolled over towards the wall with a whimper of pain.

"Draw the curtains for him, would you Vicky?" Bainbridge said to his niece and she nodded.

The colonel rested a hand on Head's shoulder.

"I will ask my friend, who is a doctor, to pay you a call," he said softly. "He is a good chap."

Head just gave another whimper.

The room had gone dark. Bainbridge and Victoria let themselves out as quietly as they could. Victoria looked bleak as she shut the door.

"Have we ruined everything for him?" she said in despair.

"No, Vicky, we did not cause the harm to Underwood that cancelled the fight, nor are we interfering in this business of the rigged match."

Victoria was not appeased.

"He thought I could help him. He believed what I said about being from a stupid consortium concerned about the welfare of boxers!"

Bainbridge took her hand and spoke his next words with care.

"Occasionally, our lies have unexpected consequences. It is why I am careful about what I masquerade as. But it was a very good lie you created. I believed it myself."

Victoria gave a weak smile.

"Could we do something for him, after all?"

"I shall ask my own physician to pay him a visit, but I suspect the matter will be taken out of our hands soon enough."

"What do you mean?" Victoria asked.

Bainbridge pulled a face.

"I do not think our friend has long for this world. His condition is worsening, and It surprises me he has lasted this long."

Victoria was obviously devastated by this news. Bainbridge squeezed her hand.

"Unfortunately, it is the way of things. We must not take it so hard."

"Life is cruel," Victoria said bitterly.

Bainbridge knew that all too well, but he was saddened to see this realisation in his niece.

"Life is life," he said. "And it must come to an end at some point. It is what we do in between that counts."

Victoria sighed, some of her old resilience returning.

"You best lean on me."

"Whatever for?" Bainbridge declared.

"Your knees, dear old uncle," Victoria rolled her eyes at him. "Remember the landlady."

"Ah!" Bainbridge did remember. The next moment he was hunched up and hobbling. "Why, oh why did I get old."

Victoria grabbed his arm.

"Do not moan too much."

"I am playing my part," Bainbridge said grandly. "My knees are such a burden upon me!"

Victoria grumbled something under her breath.

"Oh, the pain!" Bainbridge persisted, hamming things up as they went down the stairs.

"You are unbelievable," Victoria hissed.

"Really? I thought I was playing the part quite well," Bainbridge grinned at her.

"You really will have bad knees if you carry on like this," Victoria complained. "Do you have to lean on me so heavily?"

"The landlady is watching."

"Yes, but you could only pretend to be leaning on me?"

"Not so authentic."

Victoria gave another groan and attempted to smile at the landlady as they went past.

Chapter Twenty

They returned home to contemplate their next step and also because Bainbridge was hungry. As they arrived through the door, Mrs Huggins sprung on them.

"Mr Flint is in my kitchen," she declared, flapping in the way only Mrs Huggins could flap. "He seems quite beside himself. I do not know what to do with him."

"We shall speak with him," Bainbridge informed her, giving a nod to Victoria to follow him.

Mrs Huggins wrung her hands together as they travelled down the hallway.

"I know he is upset, but he is interfering with my routine. I feel I cannot get on with him about."

Bainbridge patted her arm sympathetically.

"All will be well, dear Mrs Huggins."

Mrs Huggins gave him a sad smile.

"You sounded just like Mr Fairchild right then. Oh, I still cannot fathom he is gone. It gets me right here."

She clasped a dramatic hand to her heart and a tremble entered her voice. Valiantly she soldiered on, despite clearly wanting to fall into tears.

They found Mr Flint sitting at the kitchen table, looking in a similar condition to Mrs Huggins. He had a bleak expression on his face. He stood as soon as Bainbridge entered.

"Colonel, I received news this morning that the boy is going to be charged with murder! He will go before the magistrates in a week's time and will likely be sent to Norwich prison to await his trial!"

"It surely can only be considered manslaughter?" Bainbridge said, troubled by this news. "From what the witnesses said he was in the middle of a fight at the time."

Bainbridge nearly spat the word 'witnesses'.

"Someone came forward, said they told the story wrong in the confusion," Flint said miserably. "Said they were so flustered by everything that had happened, that they were sure the police had misunderstood them. They said that the boy came after One-Foot after the fight and attacked him. That changes things, you see?"

"I do see," Bainbridge said, feeling this was his fault for revealing to Mr Ottoman that they had a witness who had seen the incident occurring in a street far removed from the scene of the fight. Clearly Ottoman had felt it prudent to revise his statement to the police, claiming he had been so distressed when first spoken to that he had made a mistake. Thus, what could have been argued to have been manslaughter was now seen as a planned attack on Underwood.

"Poor Franklin," Victoria said sorrowfully. "He has done nothing wrong."

"What can we do, Colonel?" Mr Flint looked to Bainbridge.

Bainbridge did not have an obvious answer for him.

"We have spoken to so many people," Victoria sat at the table, looking as morose as Mr Flint. "Yet, we do not know who really killed Mr Underwood."

Mrs Huggins was lurking in the background, beside herself that her table was now doubly occupied, and she was impeded in her ability to do her chores.

"We are far from finished," Bainbridge said firmly. "Certainly this is a setback, but we now know far more about Simon Underwood's life and what was going on at the time of his death. I still feel there must be a connection between his new career as a professional boxer and this crime."

"Unless this was a case of random revenge by one of his other victims," Victoria said grimly. "In which case, we shall never track them down."

Bainbridge did not tolerate despondency, not in himself, not in others. It was unproductive and self-defeating. They had a job to do and that was that.

"Someone knows," Bainbridge said firmly. "We just must find them and convince them to talk. Mr Flint, have you ever had any business with James Black?"

"Jimmy Black?" Flint pulled a face. "I thought you knew me better than that, Colonel. He is a crook."

"I appreciate that, and I am not impugning your good reputation, but sometimes we find ourselves in conference with people we would rather not be."

"I have never had dealings with him," Flint said firmly. "He knows he is not welcome at my pub."

"And he respects that?" Victoria asked the landlord.

"Oh, he does. You see, Jimmy knows better than to cross me. I have known him a very long time, and there are a lot of secrets about Jimmy I could share if I wished."

Bainbridge was intrigued.

"What sort of secrets?" he asked.

"The sort could lose a man his reputation," Flint said firmly. "Besides, he owes me a favour and he knows it."

"How could a man like Black owe you a favour?" Victoria asked, fascinated.

Flint straightened himself up as he settled in for some story telling.

"Going back to my years as a sailor, once, as a young man, I came across this fellow being beaten up by others. It looked to be going bad for him and I waded in. A sailor knows his way around a fist fight, mind. I scared off the others and rescued their victim. He was an innocuous looking person. Bit pasty and altogether too naïve. He thanked me and was going to walk off when I saw he was in a poor state and would not get far without help. So, I took him back to the boarding house I was staying in and made sure he had somewhere to sleep. Next day he awoke and said he owed me his life and he would never forget it. He told me his name was Jimmy Black, and I ought not to forget it. Naturally, I gave no more heed to his talk and went about my life, but when I opened my own pub, I soon learned of who Jimmy Black had become.

"He came to my pub just once. Told me he had not forgotten what he owed me. I said I would prefer he keep his illegal business out of my establishment, and he respected that. He never disturbs me."

"That is curious, Flint," Bainbridge said. "Every corner we turn, we seem to run into the name of Mr Black. It strikes me that somewhere in all this muddle, he is to be found at the centre."

"What does that mean?" Flint asked.

"It means, I ought to speak to him in the morning. If I can find him."

"That I cannot help you with," Flint shrugged. "I just wish I could do more for poor Franklin."

"You are doing a good deal more than most would," Bainbridge reminded him. "Now, go back to your pub and try not to fret. I have no intention of seeing Franklin go to trial for a crime he did not commit."

Flint nodded, but it was not obvious if he was truly listening. He rose from the table, politely wished them good evening, and departed through the back door. Mrs Huggins looked relieved and immediately went to reclaim her kitchen table. Victoria and Bainbridge headed to the front drawing room to discuss their next move.

"You think Jimmy Black is involved in this somehow?" Victoria asked him.

"I think that very likely," Bainbridge replied. "I am just not sure how. We shall attempt to locate him tomorrow. A good start would be The Toby Jug as we know he liked to drink there."

Bainbridge slumped into a chair with a sigh. Considering he had not walked hardly at all today, his back ached and his legs felt stiff. A vague worry surfaced in his mind that perhaps car travel was not good for the health.

Victoria sat down opposite him, staring out of a window at a warm summer's evening. She cupped her chin in one hand.

"I wonder how Mr White is?" she said softly.

Bainbridge had been endeavouring not to think of the unfortunate soul and his smoke-filled lungs. He wondered what really had occurred in that house. Had it been the pangs of a grief-stricken man that had led him to drink himself to a stupor and then drop his pipe, or had it been more about guilt? Guilt that an innocent man might hang because of the things Underwood's cronies had said. Bainbridge assumed they would never know, not with Mr White on the precipice of his own grave.

He suddenly realised that Victoria was looking at him.

"Sorry, I thought the question was rhetorical."

"I suppose it mostly was," Victoria gave a small yawn. "Well, if we are doing nothing, I shall take a little nap. I have not slept too well these last nights."

"Perhaps you are missing your own bed?" Bainbridge said with the vain hope of a man who sees the fleeting possibility of being rid of his houseguest.

"I was not sleeping at home, either," Victoria informed him firmly. "I have been thinking long and hard about my future. I believe I have come to a decision, but sometimes, when I awake in the middle of the night, doubts assail me."

"Ah," Bainbridge said. "Well, we should take heed of our doubts, sometimes they have a point."

"You shall not be rid of me so easily," Victoria informed him, then she rose and departed to her room.

Bainbridge sat for a while, enjoying the evening sunshine and the way the embrace of the chair was slowly easing his aches. As often occurred in these times of quiet

contemplation, his mind returned to Houston and a pang
of loss bit at him with the same ferocity that it had snagged
him with when he first learned his friend was dead.
Bainbridge was not sure he would ever be recovered from
that.

When the sun had dropped to an orange glow on the
horizon and the room had settled into comfortable
shadows, Bainbridge dragged himself to his feet and
walked upstairs. He did not go to his room, instead he went
two doors down and entered a completely different
chamber. Within, the curtains had been drawn, as if the
room were as much in mourning as the occupants of the
house. Bainbridge, slightly more fiercely than he needed to,
flung them open and allowed light to flood in. It was the
calming evening light, that lulls you towards a soft sort of
relaxation. A dreamy state where one's worries drift away
and instead a sort of melancholy seeps over you.

He looked at the bed in the room. Neatly made up by
Mrs Huggins, ready for an occupant who would not return.
He glanced at the nightstand beside it, a pair of cufflinks
discarded carelessly on the top, never to be retrieved. A
water glass standing empty. A watch that had wound down
without its keeper to tend it.

Beside the bed, on the rug, a pair of slippers were just
peeking out from beneath the counterpane that sagged
down to the floor. On a chair was a stack of books and
journals, recent purchases, some with their pages as yet
uncut. Upon the wardrobe door hung a Japanese theatrical
mask, which Mrs Huggins absolutely loathed and
considered evil. In Bainbridge it drew a smile to his lips.
He could recall Houston telling him the story of how he
came to have the mask and why it would never leave his
side. It brought him luck, he swore.

The smile faded. The mask had not brought Houston
luck that fateful day at the bank. Bainbridge looked around
the bedroom. Houston's bedroom. He saw so many things
that reminded him of the man – the straw boater he wore
on summer evenings. His Pinkerton certificate framed and

on the wall. The American football he swore had been handled by some famous player Bainbridge had never heard of. The favourite cigarettes. The half-read detective novel. The postcards from friends he pinned to the wallpaper.

Houston felt more alive, more real here in this room than anywhere else in the house and suddenly his presence – or was it the lack of it? – overwhelmed Bainbridge and he had to sit down sharply on the bed, a sudden shakiness making him distrust his legs.

He had not been in this room since his friend's death, he had not dared and he was not sure why he had come that evening, except that it had felt the right thing to do. He had wanted to commune with Houston's essence. It was the closest he could come to speaking with him and sharing his thoughts on the case.

"Well, Houston, this is certainly a bit of a brain teaser," he said to the air. He paused, as if awaiting a response. In reality, Bainbridge was imagining his friend talking, hearing that familiar twang as he contemplated the case along with him. Houston would be smoking, of course, Houston was always smoking.

"I don't know Julius, seems to me you have a right tricky one here."

"We have had worse, you know," Bainbridge responded to his own imagination. "Remember that one concerning the missing milk girl? We found her, did we not?"

"You found her. You trusted your gut."

"I am not sure I trust myself now," Bainbridge sighed. "I feel old, Houston, and very lost. You were my anchor."

"You have the girl, Vicky. She seems okay."

"Yes, but I miss you Houston. I miss the clarity you brought to cases."

"Is that all you miss about me? How I helped you solve cases?"

"No," Bainbridge spoke, and his voice was husky. "I miss you in many ways. The house is too quiet, and no one has pestered Mrs Huggins for coffee instead of tea. Funny how

I miss the smell of coffee, though I detested the taste."

"You always had a very English palate."

"I wish I knew what happened that day. Why you were at that bank. Were you on a case? Why did you not speak to me, tell me what you were doing?"

"Can't help you with that."

"No, no of course you cannot," Bainbridge sniffed and wiped a sneaky tear from his eye. "Probably, were you still alive, you would be as stumped as me over all this."

Bainbridge gave a slight chuckle at his weak jape.

"Still, we shall never know, shall we?"

He rose from the bed and turned to see Victoria stood in the doorway of the bedroom. She was the last person he wanted to see there, and he certainly did not want to think she had heard him speaking to himself. He had been airing his thoughts, that was all, giving them room to breathe and maybe something would come from it, some spark of insight. He had known he was not talking to Houston, after all, it had just felt good to pretend.

They stared at each other for a moment, then Victoria smiled at him, a gentle, understanding smile. She turned from the door and walked away. Bainbridge hung his head, somehow her understanding had hit him harder than if she had been worried or alarmed. Not that there was much he could do about it.

He blew his nose hard on his handkerchief and headed back downstairs, hoping dinner would not be long away.

Chapter Twenty-One

By the following morning, Bainbridge had come to a decision.

"Underwood's friends are scared," he informed Victoria. "I believe that more than ever. Ottoman was close to telling us something. If we can rattle him sufficiently, I think he will reveal himself."

Victoria listened intently. She had made no mention of what she had seen the day before when Bainbridge had been in Houston's bedroom. She was acting as if it had never happened, which unsettled Bainbridge more than if she had said something.

"This is something to do with those rigged matches?" she said.

"My gut tells me so," Bainbridge placed a hand on his substantial belly. "And a man should not ignore his gut. But, before we go to see Ottoman, I want to return to the scene of the crime and look for anything we may have missed."

"Such as?" Victoria asked.

"How can I possibly know that before I find it?"

Bainbridge replied, thinking it was obvious.

Victoria gave him a smile and went to fetch her hat. After she had left the room, he noticed a large bundle of fabric where she had been sitting. Examining it further, he discovered it was the dress she had ripped the other day which Victoria had been attempting to repair. Her efforts did not inspire confidence.

"Oh dear," Bainbridge sighed.

They loaded into the car and trundled off at a respectable pace. Bainbridge had developed a curiosity about the car's horn which was perched next to the steering wheel and drew him like a moth to a flame. He badly wanted to squeeze the bulb and hear the horn blast. He was restraining himself as he feared he would alarm the neighbourhood if he were to get carried away.

They found themselves back in Cattle Market Row. It was a little busier today, with a couple of ladies busily scrubbing their front steps and chatting to each other and small children darting about and playing a game of tag.

Bainbridge extracted himself from the car and stretched his back, both fists pressed into his flesh as he arched his spine and eased the stiffness he was feeling.

"You should do some exercise," Victoria said to him.

"My dear, you are the one who insists I must not walk anywhere," Bainbridge retorted – the word 'exercise' was equivalent to a curse word in Bainbridge's world.

Victoria gave him a look to say he knew full well what she meant and wandered up the street to the rough spot where everything had taken place.

"This is where our witness saw it happen," Victoria folded her arms and stared at the cobbles which revealed nothing to her, other than that they would benefit from a good sweep.

Bainbridge stared around him. He could not have said what he was looking for, but he would know it when he saw it. He felt a tug on his trouser leg and looked down into the round innocent eyes of a small child. The outfit and long golden hair made it difficult to determine the gender of the child, seeing as boys and girls tended to be dressed the same until they were older. He smiled at the innocent.

"Are you very old?" the child asked without any qualms about the propriety of the question.

"I am positively ancient," Bainbridge replied. "Tell me who is the oldest person in your family?"

The child creased its forehead in deep thought, swinging its arms behind its back as it gave this complicated question diligent consideration.

"My grandpa," came the answer.

"Oh, I am most certainly older than him," Bainbridge informed the innocent.

The child's eyes grew wider at this remarkable revelation and a certain hint of awe was visible. Bainbridge might as easily have said he had come from another time, that was the astonishment of the child.

"Billy! Stop pestering folk!"

A harassed mother came out of her front door to chivvy away the small child.

"He was doing no harm," Bainbridge promised the mother.

The woman, who was not much older than Victoria, tucked a loose lock of dark hair behind her ear.

"He asks so many questions," she complained of her son. "I never known a child with such questions. Drives me crazy."

"A curious mind is to be nurtured," Bainbridge reassured her.

"Hm, not when it is interfering with my work, it ain't," the woman retorted.

She took a better look at them both.

"You were here the other day."

"We were. We spoke with your neighbour concerning an incident in the street," Bainbridge replied.

"The fight?"

"I believe it was more of an attack," Bainbridge clarified. "Unfortunately, a man has since died due to the affray."

"Why does it concern you?" the woman asked, a hint of suspicion in her tone.

"Because a friend of ours has been accused of being responsible for the attack. He is wholly innocent, but we cannot prove that just now."

"Oh," the woman said, understanding. "That was a bad night. I was up with my eldest who had toothache."

"Did you happen to see outside when the incident occurred?" Bainbridge asked keenly.

The woman seemed to be staring at the cobbles, as if she could see the attack happening right there and then.

"I did," she said. "But to my way of thinking, it was a fight."

"Perhaps you could explain that to us?" Victoria asked.

The woman shrugged.

"There were four men walking along this road about where you are now, miss. They were laughing, talking, loud enough I was waiting for them to wake the whole house. My eldest was sitting by the fire, nursing her tooth. I was just stood by the window, gazing out and trying to remember my late mother's remedy for toothache. Seeing the four men distracted me for a moment. I wondered what they were about. They looked trouble and I was not in the mood for trouble. I would have given them a walloping with my broom handle if they bothered me and my family."

"It seems to me it was a good thing they were just walking by," Bainbridge said without a hint of sarcasm in his voice.

"It was," the woman said proudly. "Anyway, just as they were passing my window this fifth man ran up behind them and called out a name. I didn't hear the name, but the biggest of the four fellows turned around and this newcomer punches him one right in the belly. Well, I shot my window up at that, to tell them clear off and take their trouble elsewhere. That's when I heard the newcomer shout – 'remember who you owe, Simon!' Well, then the other fellows, the ones who had not been touched launched themselves at the newcomer and there was a scuffle. They were landing blow after blow on him and it would have gone badly, except the big fellow had sunk to the ground groaning and his mates went to help him, letting the other one escape."

The woman folded her arms, with the air of someone satisfied with themselves.

"Did you see anything else?" Bainbridge asked.

"I didn't need to see anymore. If people will get themselves into trouble, what is that to do with me? Besides, my eldest called for me then and I had more important things to concern myself with," the woman paused. "Was it the big fellow who died?"

"Yes," Bainbridge told her solemnly.

The woman thought about this for a moment.

"He didn't look good. I thought he took the blow much harder than I should expect from a big man like him. It was not as if the other guy was made of much. He took a good pounding, though, for his bother."

"Thank you, dear lady, your assistance has been much appreciated," Bainbridge said in the deeply courteous way that Victoria had noticed cast quite a spell over people. The woman, indeed, smiled and even blushed slightly.

"It was no bother, one has to help out others, don't one?" she said, attempting to sound posher than she was.

"Mum, that man is older than grandpa."

The small urchin named Billy had reappeared and was pointing at Bainbridge.

"It's rude to point," his mother slapped away his hand. "And no one can possibly be older than grandpa. He seems determined to live forever."

"But, he said…"

"Enough!" his mother upbraided him. She grabbed his arm and marched him away, all the time the protesting Billy trying to insist he had been told the absolute truth.

"Oh dear, I hope I have not earned the little fellow a smacked bottom," Bainbridge winced to Victoria.

She was not interested. She was still staring at the cobbles.

"You know what this means, Julius," she said.

"I imagine I do but let us hear your take on things."

Victoria glanced at him, trying to determine if he was mocking her. Bainbridge kept a perfectly straight face.

"How I see it," Victoria said carefully, "is that Underwood's pals got a good look at the fellow who attacked him when they went for him. That means they probably know who sent him, and the reason they refuse to tell the truth has nothing to do with them being unable to identify the real culprit behind the assault."

"I have suspected that to be the case for some time," Bainbridge agreed.

Victoria looked a little downcast at this.

"Very good deduction," Bainbridge corrected himself hastily. "You have nailed it on the head. Now, we need to rattle these liars and get them to give us a name. Preferably, the one of the real assailant."

He waddled back to the car and proceeded to scramble up.

"And while we are at it, considering you are concerned about my fitness, I suggest we buy some apples to eat."

Victoria raised an eyebrow at him.

"How will that help your fitness?"

"An apple a day keeps the doctor away!" Bainbridge said firmly. "Besides, I rather fancy one."

Victoria protested no more and soon they were motoring away, keeping their eyes peeled for the nearest fruitmonger.

By the time they found themselves before Ottoman's ironmongery shop, Bainbridge had been sated with apples. As it had happened, they had not come across a fruitmonger, but they had spied a bakery that sold apple tarts, and this had been good enough for the colonel. Three tarts later, he was feeling ready for a difficult interrogation.

"There are pastry crumbs all over my seats," Victoria muttered as he stepped to the pavement.

"I am pretty certain they are petals, not pastry," Bainbridge said haughtily.

"Petals?"

"From that bush outside the house, it sheds all over the place."

Victoria held up a scrap of pastry between two fingers.

"This is not a petal."

"We must agree to differ," Bainbridge said with a sniff and marched around the car, leaving Victoria to brush as much of his mid-morning snack as she could from her car seats.

Bainbridge entered the shop, a cheerful bell ringing over the door as he strode in. Ottoman had been in the back room and stepped to the shop front with a smile on his face, thinking he was greeting a paying customer. His face instantly fell at the sight of Bainbridge.

"What do you want?"

Bainbridge held up a hand to indicate patience.

"Please allow the lady to join us."

Ottoman scowled at him, but Bainbridge would not be swayed. A moment later Victoria hurried into the shop. She glanced at Ottoman, then at Bainbridge.

"Have I missed anything?" she asked anxiously.

"I was awaiting your arrival," the colonel assured her. "Now, Mr Ottoman…"

"I do not want to talk to either of you," Ottoman snapped. "You can get out."

Bainbridge put on a hurt expression.

"That is hardly the way to talk to people trying to seek justice for your late friend," he said.

"Justice?" Ottoman snarled at him. "You are only interested in finding a way to clear Franklin Ward's name. Well, I am having none of it. I already went to the police and revised my statement. That took some doing. I thought they were going to arrest me."

Ottoman gave a shudder at the memory.

"In any case, that is as far as I am going. You shall get no more from me," he folded his arms and did his best impression of a mute statue.

"That is very unfeeling of you," Bainbridge said. "Does

Simon Underwood deserve such little regard from you?"

"That is a trick question," Ottoman sniffed. "You are trying to get me to speak to you."

"Hardly a trick question," Bainbridge responded. "I should wish for justice for any friend of mine so cruelly snatched from this world."

"We know you saw the face of the attacker," Victoria interrupted. She was fired up, outraged for Franklin, and still annoyed over the pastry crumbs in her car. Ottoman was as good a person as any to launch her temper at. "We have spoken to someone who saw you and Stokes, and White, attacking the person. You know who the assailant is and who they work for, but you will not say anything!"

"And does that not tell you something?" Ottoman protested. "Don't you think I feel badly about it?"

"Not so badly you cannot continue to allow the police to think Franklin was the culprit," Victoria remarked. "I call that first-rate cowardice, Mr Ottoman. First-rate!"

"You can get out of my shop!" Ottoman growled. "I have had enough of you two!"

"And we have had enough of this case," Bainbridge interjected. "We want to know the truth. These lies do not sit easily on your conscience, Mr Ottoman. They sat even less easy on the shoulders of your friend, Mr White."

Ottoman's face became ashen.

"What are you saying?"

"Mr White was so appalled with himself for failing to get justice for his friend that he drank himself into a stupor and then allowed his pipe to fall to the floor," Bainbridge said, massaging the details he knew to make his point.

"You are saying he committed suicide, over it?" Ottoman gasped.

Victoria blinked.

"Oh, does that mean…?"

"Late last night," Ottoman nodded. "I went to see him. He did not seem to know who I was. Something had snapped within his mind. But… suicide?"

Ottoman clenched his teeth and pulled his hands into

fists.

"I am sorry about your friend, Mr White," Bainbridge said, his tone softening. "It is too often the case that a lie such as you, Stokes and White were complicit in, starts to consume those who have told it and causes greater misery than the thing they feared and so lied about in the first place."

Ottoman was trembling, thinking about all he had lost in the last few days. He looked around at his shop, which too might soon be lost to him. A wave of panic came over him and suddenly there seemed only one way out.

He stalked out to the back room.

"What now?" Victoria whispered to Bainbridge.

"He is coming round," Bainbridge said confidently.

At that moment they heard a loud bang.

"Good heavens! He has shot himself!" Bainbridge cried and they both darted to the back room.

Chapter
Twenty-Two

Mr Ottoman was lying groaning on the floor, cradling his left arm. He was partly obscured by a stack of boxes containing iron nails, brass house numbers and an assortment of panel pins in various lengths. He had not, in fact, shot himself. What he had been attempting to do was not obvious, but it had involved pulling something out of one of the boxes which had fallen almost on top of him. Bainbridge was not surprised at the scene, as he looked around and noted how precariously everything was stacked. It was just remarkable it had not happened sooner.

Victoria crouched beside Ottoman.

"Where are you hurt?"

"It came down on my shoulder," Ottoman indicated a sizeable iron that had tumbled from one of the boxes and was now lying innocently nearby.

Bainbridge winced. Having once had the misfortune of being caught in the stomach by a horseshoe that had just been thrown off the hoof of its former owner, he knew that hefty chunks of metal clattering into you hurt – a lot. Not without some difficulty and a good deal of alarming clicking noises, Bainbridge lowered himself into a crouch beside Ottoman as best he could.

"It could easily be broken," he said to Victoria.

Ottoman muttered a curse word.

"Manners, dear man, there is a lady present," Bainbridge told him lightly.

Ottoman bit his lip.

"It hurts!" he said pathetically. "I can't move me arm!"

"Very likely a shattered shoulder," Bainbridge mused. "Saw the same thing happen to a fellow in the army. Thrown from his horse and landed on his left shoulder. Could not move his arm for weeks."

"You ain't helping!" Ottoman cried out.

"I think we should get him to his feet," Victoria suggested.

"Yes! Please!" Ottoman begged.

Bainbridge had enough troubling getting himself up, so abstained from assisting Ottoman to his feet. Instead, he made a valiant, if not entirely productive attempt to move the fallen boxes and restore their contents. If nothing else, he had shown he was willing to help.

Victoria proved to have more strength in her than might have been supposed. She got her hand under Ottoman's good arm and hefted him up. He whimpered and sobbed as she pulled at him.

"Are your legs broken?" she demanded.

"No," he sniffed.

"Then you can use them and help yourself, I cannot lift a grown man alone."

Snuffling to himself about how cruel some people could be, Ottoman begrudgingly mastered his legs and hobbled into a stand.

"Have you a sitting room or something?" Victoria asked him.

"Through that other door," Ottoman said, with a vague

wave of his good arm.

The 'other door' proved to lead from the shop, so they had to leave the back room and step behind the counter before entering a snug little kitchen. A door at the back of the room was ajar and revealed a tight set of stairs leading up, presumably, to Ottoman's bedroom. Victoria settled the man in a tatty armchair near the kitchen range and then attempted to fathom out how you made tea. She had a rough idea it required water to be boiled and tea leaves, but the practical side of things eluded her. She had always had her tea brought to her in a teapot, its mysterious brewing process conducted somewhere out-of-sight in the kitchens of her mother's house.

Bainbridge, seeing her uncertainty about what to do with the kettle she had found on the range, sallied forth finally feeling he had a purpose he could fulfil. If there was one thing he was capable of, it was making tea.

"Many a time on campaign I whipped up a brew for myself and my comrades," he informed them cheerily. "English tea is a Godsend when you are contemplating a bloody march on the enemy."

Ottoman snivelled to himself.

"Good thing you do not have many customers, so we can take the time to tend to you," Victoria said artlessly.

"That's it, rub it in!" Ottoman wailed. "My business is failing! No one wants what I sell! I overspent on brass house numbers that no one is buying! Before long this whole place will be gone, and I shall not have a roof over my head."

"Oh," Victoria said, realising her error. She glanced to Bainbridge hopefully, but he had nothing to offer her.

"It has all gone horribly wrong and just when there was hope around the corner, that was snatched from me too!"

"You are referring to the big bet Underwood had placed on himself in the fight to come?" Victoria asked.

"I invested every last penny I had on that bet. I was going to make a fortune. Maybe I would have changed this place from an ironmongers to something else, something people want. I don't know, but it would have been better. And now Simon is dead, and I can't get my money for the bet back. I tried, but they refuse."

Ottoman rubbed at his nose with the back of his hand, a forlorn creature lost in his own misery.

"We should put that arm in a sling," Bainbridge suggested. "Can you move your fingers, Ottoman?"

Ottoman made a rude sign at him with the fingers of his good hand.

"I did mean the injured arm," Bainbridge sighed, not taking offence. "If you can move your fingers, your shoulder is probably not dislocated."

Whimpering, Ottoman flexed his fingers.

"It hurts!"

"I rather fancy that is a good sign," Bainbridge said to him brightly. "A sling is the thing. It will keep your arm steady as it heals."

Ottoman was wallowing in self-pity again.

"Why did it have to fall on my right shoulder? I do everything with my right hand!"

Bainbridge had nothing to say to that. He could not change what had occurred, nor answer why bad luck sometimes conspired against you. He busied himself with the kettle which was slowly coming to a boil.

"What we need is a long strip of cloth," he told Victoria.

She went off in search of something suitable, rather glad to be away from the whining of Ottoman.

"I am done for now!" Ottoman said pathetically.

"That is hardly the right attitude for this situation," Bainbridge scolded him gently. "Yes, it is a setback, but one has to make the best of things. You are not dead, after all."

"I might as well be. When I am out on the street not a penny to my name, I might as well be dead."

"I am beginning to see why your business has failed, if you are always so negative about everything," Bainbridge said to him in a fiercer tone. "You cannot just sit back and allow life to happen. You must get out there and make a difference. Drum up trade for your shop."

"I tried," Ottoman griped. "That is why I bought the brass house numbers!"

"And have you advertised the fact?" Bainbridge asked him. "I saw nothing in your window to suggest you sold brass house numbers. People cannot buy what they do not know about."

Ottoman sniffed, his gaze wandering to the front of his shop.

"You need a display out there to draw people in. Wash your windows and move some of the stands so people can see inside. Make yourself welcoming. Go around to places that might need ironmongery and advertise yourself. Offer a discount for purchases over a certain amount, or for repeat customers. Get your name known!"

Ottoman's misery had lifted as he listened to Bainbridge and saw possibilities opening up before him.

"You think I could make this business profitable?" he asked.

"I think you would be a damn fool not to try," Bainbridge informed him. "If you do everything you can and still this place goes under, well, at least you know you did your very best and that is all anyone can ask of themselves. If you just sit here and allow it to slip from you, you were not worthy of it in the first place."

"You are right!" Ottoman said a new light illuminating his eyes. He was a little feverish from the shock he had just had and was riding a wave of adrenaline, yet suddenly there seemed to be a light at the end of the tunnel.

Victoria returned with a long strip of cloth which she presented to Bainbridge. He demonstrated how the injured arm should be hoisted up into a sling to keep it still while it healed.

"There, it will be inconvenient, Mr Ottoman, but use this time wisely. Go about making contacts and promoting your wares. Invest a little effort and with luck you shall have a good return."

Ottoman tentatively touched his injured arm.

"Luck has never been my friend," he said, his pessimism

returning.

"Luck, I have always found, is very dependent on perspective," Victoria mused. "Take the man who is drowning and is thrown a line, but in the process of being hauled ashore he catches his foot and breaks his ankle. If he is of a positive nature he shall arrive on land and say to himself 'what good luck that I was saved from drowning with only a broken ankle to show from my misadventure.' If he is of a pessimistic nature he shall say 'what bad luck that not only have I nearly drowned today, but I broke my ankle too'."

Ottoman listened thoughtfully.

"Simon always said you made your own luck," he mumbled.

He touched his arm again.

"You have been very kind to me, considering how rude I have been," he averted his eyes from his guests.

"We could not have left you there," Bainbridge said firmly.

Ottoman was considering his situation and revising some of his earlier doggedness about telling Bainbridge and Victoria what he knew. He felt he owed them something, after what they had done for him. He also recalled something his mother used to say, that a good deed done today brought dividends tomorrow. He had always thought it was nonsense, but looking back on his life, the only thing that his bad deeds had brought him was misfortune and unhappiness. It could be worth giving his mother's old motto a try.

After all, he did feel bad about what had happened to Simon and he wanted some better sort of justice for him than a random man being blamed for his attack. Ottoman fixed his attention on Bainbridge.

"It was Stokes who convinced me and White not to say what we knew about that night."

"What did you know that he wanted to hide?"

"The man who attacked Simon, his name is Archie Gubbins. He is a street rat, pure and simple. In a fair fight

Simon would have made him into mash!"

Ottoman jutted out his chin, offended at the thought of how his friend had been taken by surprise and not allowed to defend himself.

"Why was Stokes so concerned about you telling the police the man's name?" Victoria asked.

Ottoman looked uneasy.

"I don't actually know. He made it really plain that it was important we did not say the man's name to anyone, but he never explained why. Stokes was always more involved with Simon's dealings than me or White. We had our own work to get on with, while Stokes was always with Simon. He was like his back-up."

"Then Stokes probably knows exactly why this attack occurred," Bainbridge groaned to himself, thinking of the trouble they would have to go to if they were to get anything out of Stokes. The man was unlikely to give up information willingly.

"White felt really bad about it," Ottoman became solemn. "He felt we had done wrong by Simon. Before he died, Simon had demanded we get revenge for him. He knew he was short for this world. We vowed we would, but we all knew we were not going to. The moment he was dead, and questions started to be asked, Stokes was hammering it into us that we did not mention Archie's name. He was quite scary about it. Threatened us a little."

Ottoman frowned, thinking of his supposed friend waving a fist at him and berating White for wanting to tell the truth.

"He said he would do for us if we breathed the truth, and I believed him," Ottoman swallowed. "I never really liked him you know, now I come to think about it. He had this nasty streak to him. He was fine when Simon was present, but I would not want to be alone in his company."

Ottoman was looking very worried now.

"If he discovers I told you…"

"He shall not hear that from us," Bainbridge reassured him.

Ottoman nodded his head. It was too late to take it back anyway.

"What will you do now?" he asked.

"Where can we find Archie Gubbins?" Bainbridge asked him.

Ottoman gave this due thought.

"You can sometimes find him in the graveyard of St Julian's. He knows a secret way into the old crypt. He lives there."

"Charming," Victoria said.

"What else do you know about Mr Gubbins?" Bainbridge asked.

Ottoman shrugged his shoulders without thinking and cried out in pain. Tears formed at the corners of his eyes and he nearly sobbed.

"I don't know anything much about him. He is just another guttersnipe who takes money for jobs no one else wants. Why do you think he was the one going after Simon? No one else was stupid enough to try it," Ottoman growled at the pain. "Now, leave me alone, will you?"

Bainbridge knew they were done here. He presented Ottoman with the tea he had made him then, with well wishes for his recovery, he and Victoria departed.

Outside, on the pavement, they contemplated their next move.

"St Julian's?" Victoria said anxiously.

"It is in a terrible state of repair. They have been raising money to restore it for decades," Bainbridge replied, then he caught the edge to her voice. "You are not concerned about going to a graveyard, are you?"

"Of course not!" Victoria said, pulling herself up tall to deter his curious gaze.

She marched towards the car. Bainbridge followed just behind, wondering quite what he had accidentally tapped into just then.

"What are we going to do about Stokes?" Victoria asked as he climbed up in the seat next to her.

"He is a problem for another day. I have deep concerns about him and just what he was prepared to do to keep the truth from us."

"What does that mean?"

Bainbridge frowned.

"I am rather afraid it means something quite bad."

Chapter
Twenty-Three

St Julian's was a very ancient church built in the eleventh and twelfth centuries, one of the fifty-eight churches constructed in Norwich immediately after the Norman Conquest. It was dedicated to either Julian the Hospitaller, or Julian of Le Mans, no one was quite sure which, but both were Roman Catholic saints. In the fourteenth century, Lady Julian of Norwich, an anchoress (a sort of religious hermit) had her anchoresses' cell in the churchyard.

The later centuries had been hard on the church and only fifty or so years earlier the place was so ruinous the east wall had fallen down. Attempts were being made to restore it but were dogged by funding issues. It had partly been repaired, yet still looked little more than rubble in places. As they pulled up outside the graveyard, Victoria shuddered.

"What is this fear you have of churches?" Bainbridge asked her as he descended from the car.

"Not churches. I have nothing against churches," Victoria corrected him. "Churches can be very lovely places. It is just they tend to be surrounded by dead people."

Victoria's eyes had fallen on the many gravestones and slab tombs in the churchyard, most jerking out of the ground at odd angles and so weathered it would be impossible to read what was on them. Bainbridge came to a sharp stop.

"You appreciate, my dear, the line of work I am in?"

Victoria gave him an odd look.

"You are a detective," she said, thinking he was being foolish.

"Yes, and very often I am called to investigate the sudden death of a person that is not seen as natural or accidental."

"I understand that," Victoria said, annoyed at his tone. "That is why we are here, because Simon Underwood is dead."

"Quite. But what I really mean is that quite often this business of mine involves dead people, in one state or another and, in my experience, it is quite common for one to find oneself looking upon the said dead person at some point."

Victoria had no expression on her face.

"But you are solving crimes, why would you go anywhere near a dead person?"

"Sometimes it is necessary," Bainbridge had one hand on the gate into the churchyard. "Sometimes it just happens."

"Well, we shall have to agree that remains your business and I shall be more of the research and scholarly deduction side of things."

Bainbridge shook his head, but he opted not to correct her. She would learn in time. Perhaps it would be her first body that would convince her to stop playing detective and he would be left alone. Oddly, this thought brought a pang to Bainbridge's chest and it occurred to him he would actually miss Victoria if she were to leave.

They walked towards the church, Victoria looking uneasily at the graves either side of the path. A lot of them had skulls and crossbones ornamenting them. This was, after all, a very old church and people in the past were blunter about death than today's folk who preferred cherubs and angels upon their tombs. Bainbridge thought he might quite like a skull and crossbones on his headstone, just to remind everybody what was coming for them and that they ought to behave themselves.

Strangely cheered by this thought, he paused at the church door where a carefully handwritten notice informed people the door was locked and the church, due to safety concerns, was not open to the public, but that they were free to wander the graveyard. Bainbridge would have felt free to wander the graveyard had he been allowed to or not.

"I think it is bones that bother me," Victoria said behind him. "Skulls and bones. Though, of course, skulls are bones, but one tends to think of them separately."

"Have you had many encounters with bones?" Bainbridge asked her, trying to keep a smile off his face.

"I remember, when I was a little girl, we had a trip to Rome. My mother wished to see all the Catholic churches and their relics."

"Your mother always was interested in things like that. A touch morbid for my mind," Bainbridge sniffed.

"We went to this one church where they had the body of a saint. I do not recall the name of the saint, but I do remember she – or perhaps it was he – was on display in a glass case. The body had rotted away, but there was this skeleton dressed in a white robe and there was fair hair still attached to the skull. I screamed so hard at the sight I fainted. I had nightmares for weeks."

"The good news is that around here everyone who has passed on is securely buried in the earth," Bainbridge informed her, waving at a nearby grave. "While it is always possible for a stray bone to appear, it is quite unlikely."

Victoria was not convinced and picked her way along

the path with care, lest suddenly an arm or leg bone were to spring or slide in front of her.

"This appears to be the place Mr Gubbins is living," Bainbridge had found a section of wall that had fallen down, exposing a narrow space below ground level which appeared to have once been part of the church crypt. They could see stone walls and broken tombstones, but fortunately no bones. On the floor of the crypt was a thin mattress, little more than a padded blanket and next to it was an unlit oil lamp and an old biscuit box, wrapped up with a thin chain and padlocked. That was all the worldly possessions of Archie Gubbins.

"Poor soul," Bainbridge reflected to himself. "Well, he is not here, but he shall return. I suggest we wait."

There were some large lumps of masonry stone near the hole and Bainbridge settled himself on the nearest one with a groan.

"That's better."

Victoria peered anxiously into the crypt, partly wanting to see a bone just to test her nerve, and partly horrified at the thought. She did not see anything untoward.

"I imagine that as part of the restorations they have secured all the loose bones and buried them with respect," Bainbridge informed her. "It is the right thing to do, after all."

Victoria was still eyeing the dim space. With reluctance, she came and sat beside Bainbridge. It was by necessity that she found herself nearest the graves, which were still causing her alarm. Every time she looked at one, she found herself thinking about the body that might be just beneath the surface. She pictured bones in dresses and suits, smiling skulls leering at her and a chill ran up and down her flesh. She dragged her eyes from the stone.

"I do hope he arrives soon."

They sat for a while each contemplating their own thoughts. Bainbridge had discovered a tiny tin of mints in his pocket he had forgotten about and happily settled to sucking on one. He offered the tin to Victoria, but she turned him down.

"Explain to me properly what you meant about Stokes being prepared to do anything to hide the truth," she said after a while.

"I have nothing certain on the matter," Bainbridge explained to her. "But it seemed to me that Stokes was very, very keen that his companions should keep their mouths shut. Keener than might seem reasonable. And Ottoman said he threatened them."

"I still do not see what you are saying," Victoria frowned.

Bainbridge scratched at his moustache and debated having another mint as he carried on.

"Ottoman said White was not happy. He was the loose link in their chain of three. Supposing Stokes decided he was too dangerous to leave alive, that he could bring a lot of trouble down onto their heads if he spoke out?"

"Yes, but all White knew was that this man Gubbins attacked Underwood. He hardly seems a man Stokes would be worried about."

"Ah, but you forget his little message," Bainbridge held up a finger. "He said 'Remember who you owe!' Well, he was not referring to himself in that matter. It is hardly feasible Underwood owed him anything and a threat from Gubbins alone is unlikely to have shaken the big man. No, it was a message from someone else, someone powerful who preferred not to get their hands dirty."

"And it is this person, not Gubbins, that Stokes is scared of," Victoria elaborated.

"Exactly. Stokes knows all about Underwood's business. Ottoman told us he was with him all the time. He would know who he might owe, and it was obviously someone that scared Stokes. He feared that if White or Ottoman revealed to the police that Gubbins had attacked Underwood, then it would only be a matter of time before the police found him. Gubbins would likely state who he had been employed by and Stokes feared that person would be furious at him for speaking out and would come after him. It was safer, therefore, to say nothing."

"Who do you think this person might be?" Victoria asked.

"I have a hunch," Bainbridge informed her. "I just do not understand the 'why' of it as yet. I must be missing something."

As they had been talking, the air had grown cooler and Victoria felt a splatter of wetness on her cheek that drew her attention sharply to the sky. Grey clouds had rolled in and when she put out her hand, denuded of her driving glove, she felt a raindrop on her palm.

"We should retreat to the car!" she declared.

"Bother to that. We will never catch Gubbins from the car. He could come from any direction into this graveyard."

"Then what do you suggest?" Victoria said crossly, tucking her hair into her hat as fast as she could.

Bainbridge paused for a moment, thinking, then his attention wandered to the exposed crypt.

"Oh no!" Victoria warned him.

"It is dry inside," Bainbridge countered. "And we shall be perfectly placed for Gubbins' return."

"I am not going down into a crypt!" Victoria protested, but Bainbridge had already got up and was inspecting the opening, tapping his stick against the stonework.

"Seems very stable," he said. "And it is easy enough to clamber down this rubble."

"Julius!" Victoria cried out helplessly as Bainbridge started to disappear into the crypt.

She looked around hopelessly for some alternative to this ridiculous notion, then gave a gasp of annoyance as the rain started to pour. Seeing how she would be soaked by the time she reached the car, she gave in to the inevitable and descended into the crypt. Bainbridge was correct that the stone and rubble had formed a comfortable slope into the space, and she did not fall or slip on the way down. Once inside, she took off her hat and shook water from it.

"Do mind poor Mr Gubbins' bed," Bainbridge scolded

her.

Victoria looked down and to her horror she was stood right upon the flimsy mattress and had shook rainwater onto it. Feeling terrible that she had trampled Gubbins' crude bed, she hopped away and joined Bainbridge by the back wall. He had found another lump of fallen masonry to sit upon.

"What if Gubbins does not want to talk to us?" Victoria said to him.

"I have a hunch Gubbins is the sort who spills his guts at the slightest provocation," Bainbridge replied. "You recall what Ottoman said about him? He was the only one fool enough to do the job."

It was then they heard footsteps crunching on the stony path outside the church. Someone was hurrying to get out of the rain. Bainbridge put a finger to his mouth to indicate, quite unnecessarily in Victoria's opinion, that they ought to remain silent.

The hole into the crypt grew darker as someone blocked out the light and then a person tumbled in, rushing so fast out of the rain they did not see that they had guests. The person was about seventeen or eighteen, small for his age. He flapped rain off his coat and only then did he notice his two visitors.

There was a still moment when everyone stared at each other, then Bainbridge wagged his stick at the crypt entrance.

"It was raining," he said. "And the church is locked."

"Oh," said the youth.

He was sporting a number of bruises to his face and now Victoria looked closer she could she he was holding his side and favouring his left leg.

"Been in the wars?" Victoria asked him.

The youth gave her a quick look, then eased himself down onto a lump of stone.

"Been a rough few days," he said.

"For a few people," Bainbridge said calmly. "Tell me,

had you heard that Simon One-Foot was dead, Archie?"

Archie looked up sharply with an expression of horror. He started to get up.

"Honestly, if you run, I cannot follow you and I shall not follow you," Bainbridge told him. "I am rather hoping you might be community minded instead, seeing how another man has been accused of landing the blow on Simon that killed him in your place. Have you heard of the term scapegoat?"

Archie was up on his feet, but he did not look in much of a state to flee.

"Stokes and his companions gave you quite a pounding for your trouble. I hope you were paid well for your effort."

Archie was torn with indecision. He didn't feel particularly threatened by this older gentleman and his lady friend, who looked like they were just out for a bit of sightseeing. It seemed a shame to go get wet just to run away from these two when they were causing him no real bother. He was also very sore from his beating and running was not something that appealed to him at that moment. He came to a decision and sat down again.

"It paid for a meal," he said with the sort of air that suggested what more could he expect?

"I would like to know who hired you," Bainbridge said.

Archie gave him a humourless grin.

"I don't need that sort of trouble."

"Of course," Bainbridge nodded. "That is understandable. However, you are in a difficult position Mr Gubbins, what with three witnesses being able to place you at the scene of the crime."

"What?" Gubbins looked horrified.

"Yes, three witnesses. It would have been four, but Mr White has suffered a misfortune. However, his companions have been quite forthcoming. I therefore have more than enough information to go directly to the police and accuse you."

"No!" Gubbins declared.

"I would prefer not to. You are not the real culprit in this affair, not at the heart of it. I want your employer not you."

Gubbins might not be bright, but he was quick-witted, and he saw where Bainbridge was headed.

"I tell you who hired me, you will leave me be?"

"That seems reasonable," Bainbridge concurred.

Gubbins took a deep breath, wincing at his bruised ribs.

"All right then. I'll tell you, but I don't see how it will do you any good."

Chapter
Twenty-Four

They arrived back at the police station with news that was not going to best please Inspector Dougal. They were allowed to go straight to his office where they found him pulling a piece of string across the room from where it was fastened to a drawing pin in the far wall.

"Hello," he said. "I do not suppose you could hold this?"

He held out the string to Victoria and she took hold of it helpfully.

"What is this?" Bainbridge asked conversationally.

"Trying to work out the necessary trajectory for a pistol shot to have been fired from that point there to hit a man standing about where Miss Victoria is in the chest."

He played with the string until it was taut and exactly where he wanted it.

"As I suspected," he said. "The angle is impossible."

Murmuring to himself, Dougal took the string from Victoria and started to roll it up around his hand.

"The shooter could have been pointing down," Bainbridge suggested to him.

"Oh no, he was shot through a partition wall and we have the bullet hole to confirm the angle," Dougal told him cheerfully. "We have been told it was an accident. I suspect otherwise, now, how can I help you?"

"We have news about who killed Simon Underwood," Victoria said, stepping towards the inspector's desk.

Dougal was trying to pull the drawing pin from the wall.

"Do you have a culprit?" he asked keenly.

"We have the person who caused his death and the person who is really responsible. However, I do not yet know the motive for the crime, and I am not sure I have the evidence to prove our case," Bainbridge replied.

Inspector Dougal looked disappointed by this news.

"Well, tell me anyway and we can think about the rest later."

"The person who delivered the fatal punch to Mr Underwood is Archie Gubbins," Bainbridge explained. "I tell you this name in complete confidence, as I have informed Archie that in exchange for his cooperation, I would not get him into trouble with the police."

"I know of Archie. He has walked through the doors of this station many a time. Not a bad sort, but his circumstances and the people he associates with tend to lead him into bad habits. So, he punched Underwood?"

"Yes, but he had no intention of killing him," Bainbridge replied. "I do not doubt he considered himself a woeful match for the big man, but he was prepared to take a chance for the money he was being offered and no one else was fool enough to make the attempt."

"Gubbins took a severe beating off Underwood's cronies for his troubles," Victoria added. "They would probably have killed him had Underwood not drawn their attention by his condition."

"I understand," Dougal smiled at her. "You are saying Gubbins may have launched the blow but the person who is guilty of murder is actually the one who directed him. Arresting Gubbins would solve the crime and release Franklin, but it would not be real justice."

"Exactly," Victoria said firmly. "Gubbins was just a messenger boy, at the end of the day."

"Then, who hired him?" Dougal asked.

"A very good question," Bainbridge nodded. "And I should not have received an answer to that very question without the assistance of Gubbins."

"I appreciate what you are saying," Dougal held up a hand to indicate Bainbridge need not hammer home the point. "As far as I am concerned, I have never heard the name Gubbins in connection with this case."

"Good," Bainbridge said. "For the one who is really responsible for all this is Jimmy Black."

There was a pause as this sank in. Dougal nodded to himself.

"I cannot say I am entirely surprised. His name has been circulating around this case for a while. But why did he have Gubbins go after Underwood? It was a threat, I imagine."

"Truthfully, I do not know the reason. Gubbins, as might be expected, also did not know the reason. Black was asking around for someone to do a job for him. No one else wanted it when it reached Gubbins' ears. He was prepared to give it a go for the benefit of enough money for a hot meal."

"It seems appalling that he took such a risk, ended up beaten black and blue, and killed a man all for a single hot meal," Victoria sighed.

Dougal and Bainbridge exchanged a look. Perhaps they had been involved in the criminal world too long, for nothing much surprised them, certainly not what people would do for ridiculously small sums of money.

"Along with punching Underwood, Gubbins was to shout out a message," Bainbridge continued. "He was to say, 'Remember who you owe!' Or something along those lines. Gubbins was a bit hazy on that point. In any case, he was to make it plain to Underwood that this was a threat and presumably the message would have been enough to indicate who was sending the warning."

"It was certainly enough for Stokes who became fearful of reporting what really occurred to the police after Underwood's death," Victoria added. "He was so concerned, that he did not even want the police to learn who had thrown the deadly punch, for fear that Gubbins would then tell everything to you, Inspector, and Jimmy Black would wrongly assume Stokes and his cohorts had revealed him."

"As it happened, he would have been utterly correct about Gubbins," Bainbridge said.

"This is all very well," Dougal spoke, "but I have nothing upon which to base an arrest of Jimmy Black. Gubbins is not available to me to act as a witness and you have offered me nothing else to point to the man, not even a motive. At this juncture, it is not enough for me to release Franklin from our cells."

Victoria was about to say something sharp. Bainbridge butted in.

"I know, your hands are tied in his matter. That is why we must think about things in another way."

"Go on," Dougal said. "If you have a plan, I will gladly assist you in any way I can."

Bainbridge stood a little taller as he made his proposition.

"There is only one potential weak link in all of this," he said. "Stokes. And as weaknesses go, it is not much. From what I have learned, Stokes was heavily involved in Underwood's business. He was with him all the time, presumably took a cut from the gambling associated with Underwood's matches. He knew everything that was going on in Underwood's world, including who he had upset.

"Stokes suspected, if not outright knew, that the warning from Gubbins had really come from Jimmy Black. That was why he insisted to the others that they must only give one name to the police, the name of Franklin Ward who would make a perfect scapegoat. He threatened them, in fact, to keep the secret. Stokes, therefore, could be our witness, if he could be persuaded to speak out."

"That sounds unlikely," Dougal frowned. "If Stokes is that determined to avoid Jimmy Black's attention, why would he speak out against him."

"Honestly, it is not an easy situation," Bainbridge agreed. "The only hope we have of getting Stokes to confess is if we make it of benefit to him."

Dougal was troubled by this.

"I do not know if that is possible."

"It is a longshot, that I will not deny. But when the only other option is to see Franklin on trial for a murder he did not commit, I shall try anything."

Victoria glanced at her uncle. This plan was new to her as well.

"What are you saying?" she asked.

"Stokes, at the worst, might do prison time for lying to the police," Bainbridge continued. "But, if he was found guilty of murder, he would hang, for certain."

"Murder?" Dougal said. "How is Stokes guilty of murder?"

"Possibly he is not," Bainbridge said. "Proving Franklin innocent and getting Stokes to talk, rather relies on a hunch I have that he has bloodied his own hands out of fear."

"How good a hunch?" Dougal asked dubiously.

"The sort that has got me out of trouble in the past," Bainbridge reassured him. "You recall I said Stokes had threatened his friends into silence? Well, we now know that in the case of Mr White, that silence was imperfect. White felt guilty at letting his deceased friend down. He was not sure about telling lies that resulted in the arrest of an innocent man. In short, he was considering telling the truth and Stokes knew this.

"My supposition is admittedly slightly farfetched. I have no evidence for it except for that fact that everyone was very confused by White's sudden drinking bout. He was considered a reformed drinker and the amount of alcohol in his front room indicated a quite serious amount of consumption – the sort that might even kill a person no longer accustomed to it."

"What is this?" Dougal asked, confused.

"Ah, we may not have explained about the fire," Victoria said to her uncle.

Bainbridge shook his head at his own failure and rectified the situation by elaborating on the strange scene they had stumbled upon.

"To all intents and purposes, it looked like a drunken accident," he said. "White drank himself silly and then dropped his lit pipe. It happens, after all. But here is my problem. First White was no longer a drinker, he had been abstaining from alcohol for some years. As a result, he could not have consumed the amount of alcohol as indicated by the bottles found in his front room. Second, something that has concerned me, is that the pipe apparently set light to the carpet. Pipes, of course, can drop and spill hot ash, but they are not as great a risk as say a dropped match or even a cigarette. I have smoked more than one pipe in my time, and I can tell you how annoying it is when you drop one and all the tobacco spills out. More often than not, it goes out at once."

"Unusual coincidences do sometimes occur," Dougal shrugged.

"Yes, but that brings me to my third concern. The fire spread rapidly in a room with limited combustibles. The fire chief I spoke to suggested the alcohol had acted as an accelerant. Alcohol does certainly burn well, but often too fast and furious. It started to occur to me that if someone wanted that fire to really burn well, maybe they poured plenty of alcohol on the carpet and the chair, maybe even the curtains. The evidence would be consumed in the flames and everyone would just assume White drunk himself into a stupor and set his own house on fire."

"It is a nice theory," Dougal said. "But you have no proof for any of it."

"No," Bainbridge agreed. "I have a hunch. A hunch that Stokes was worried about Mr White's conscience and wanted to be rid of him."

Dougal sat back in his chair and mulled all this over.

"I generally trust your hunches," he told Bainbridge, "but this one is too farfetched."

"Stokes never went to visit White after the fire," Victoria quickly added. "Ottoman had been to see him. He told us so. Not Stokes."

"Maybe Stokes did not know about the fire," Dougal suggested.

"Or he knew, but he was not prepared to find out if White remembered what had occurred," Victoria countered.

Dougal tapped his fingers on the table.

"White is dead. We cannot ask him about this," he sighed.

"No," Bainbridge nodded. "That is where my plan comes into play. If Stokes can be convinced that we know he set fire to White's house, then he might just be prepared to speak out against Black to avoid a murder charge."

"You mean, lie to him to convince him we know something and then make a bargain?" Dougal said dubiously.

"The reality is we cannot have him charged for the murder of White on the little evidence I have, which is nothing. We can, however, nail Black if Stokes will speak and thus save the life of Franklin. It is a gamble, but worth a shot."

Dougal was thinking carefully.

"What if your hunch is wrong and Stokes had nothing to do with White's death?"

"Then, I do not know what to do," Bainbridge admitted.

Dougal considered this all for a long time. Making Victoria look to her uncle anxiously. She had not heard this plan before, and she had to admit she was unconvinced by its potential. Stokes had seemed a hard, resilient man who would not be easily swayed. Then there was the plausibility of Bainbridge's theory, which did not inspire her either. All told, she was dubious about his plan and would not have been surprised if Dougal simply turned down the idea.

In fact, when the inspector did finally speak, his reply caused her more consternation because it was not what she expected.

"Bainbridge, I have seen how your hunches pan out before. I shall take your word on this one and hope for the best," Dougal said, standing from his chair. "What do you want me to do?"

"You shall be nearby, ready to provide an escort for Mr Stokes, should my plan succeed," Bainbridge explained. "If it fails, well, you shall not be needed at all."

That made them sombre for a moment. They were really going out on a limb for Bainbridge and they all knew it.

"We must remember we are doing this for Franklin," Victoria said softly after the silence had dragged on for a while.

"Yes, of course, my dear," Dougal smiled at her. "If all this world needed for good to triumph was noble intentions, then we should be in a far happier land."

Victoria was not sure if he was mocking her or not. She had meant the words to cheer them and strengthen their resolve, instead she felt as if they were treating her as naïve. She had felt that way a lot around Bainbridge, knowing that sometimes she was limited in her knowledge and her understanding of the world, but she did not appreciate it from the inspector. She pursed her lips.

"Then, perhaps we should not try at all?" Victoria countered him crossly.

"I think that would be a shame, for Franklin's sake," Dougal said, a little puzzled by her tone. "Shall we head out?"

He grabbed his hat and motioned to the door. Victoria stuck out her chin and held her head high as the gentlemen waited politely for her to go through first. She felt as if she had made a misstep but was not sure how or why. Feeling more baffled than ever and concerned she had been rude to Dougal for no reason, she led the way downstairs.

Chapter
Twenty-Five

Venturing back into Stokes' domain caused mild trepidation in Bainbridge. Not because he was afraid of the man – he had seen surlier beasts in his time in the army, quite often they happened to be in the form of an upstart sergeant-major – he was anxious because of the gamble he was about to attempt. Not to put too fine a point on it, but this may be the only way to save Franklin and if it went wrong, he really did not know what he could do. He kept all this to himself naturally and endeavoured to appear confident and determined as they brushed past Stokes' tetchy landlord and descended to his basement accommodation.

"Mr Stokes?" Bainbridge knocked on the man's door with the head of his walking stick. Victoria loitered just behind, she recalled what they had seen the last time they had been here. "Stokes?"

The landlord was stood in the doorway onto the stairs

that led down, muttering to himself about rude posh folks who lacked common decency.

"Stokes!" Bainbridge demanded through the door, his patience wearing thin. "For heaven's sake, open this…"

The door swung open and Bainbridge nearly tumbled through it. Stokes gave him an evil look. He had not improved during the couple of days since they had last seen him, in fact, he looked a tad worse for wear. This, Bainbridge considered, was understandable as the man had clearly been walking in the shadow of Simon Underwood, building his life and his financial stability around him. Without Underwood, he was lost.

"What do you want?" Stokes demanded in a tone that was designed to be nasty and suggest painful things were possible in response to Bainbridge's next few words.

Bainbridge was neither intimidated nor particularly impressed. It was the fact that Stokes was wearing carpet slippers and had forgotten to do up the buttons of his trousers that changed the image from something threatening, to something rather sad and comical.

"We need to talk," Bainbridge explained.

"Fine," Stokes folded his arms, demonstrating that he had no intention of letting them into his room. "We shall talk here."

"If you say so," Bainbridge replied conversationally. "I thought you might prefer somewhere more private in consideration of what we are to discuss."

"If this is about Franklin Ward, I already told you. I saw him as plain as day swing at Simon."

"Yes, yes, Mr Stokes, that you have made completely clear. That is not why I am here. I wish to talk about Mr White."

Stokes hesitated. Victoria felt a flicker of hope rise in her as she saw the look on his face. Maybe, just maybe, this peculiar and risky scheme would work.

"White? What about White?" Stokes snarled.

"You are, of course, aware he is dead?"

Stokes had that nasty look on his face again.

"What is your point?"

Without giving the man time to compose himself too much, Bainbridge blustered on.

"You are presumably also aware of the terrible fire that heralded Mr White's demise?"

Stokes huffed; it was the closest they were going to get to a confirmation.

"And you might also be aware that White did not die at once, that he lingered for a couple of days. Long enough for both ourselves and your friend Ottoman to pay him a visit and ask what happened to him."

Stokes' eyes flicked to his landlord on the stairs. It was enough to tell Bainbridge he was onto something.

"Clear off you old eavesdropper!" Stokes yelled at his landlord over the head of Bainbridge.

"I think I should stay. I think I should listen to this!" the landlord countered.

"Clear off if you know what is good for you!" Stokes wagged his fist at the man and his landlord thought better of his defiance and scarpered.

Stokes turned his attention back to Bainbridge.

"Why do you want to talk about White?" he asked, pretending he was unconcerned.

Bainbridge felt his metaphorical snare tightening, but he had to hold his nerve.

"I think you know as well as I do that Mr White did not perish as the consequence of a drinking binge. He was not considered to be a heavy drinker by either his neighbours or your friend Ottoman, who, I might add, was very troubled by the circumstances of White's death. White was taken in by his neighbours after the fire. We went to see him, and he was able to tell us what really happened that day."

Stokes had lost some of his colour. Bainbridge was waiting for him to slam the door in his face, but it did not come. Stokes was calculating what Bainbridge might know and how serious that might be for him.

"White had a conscience. It was a failing in your eyes.

He was troubled that he had lied to the police and that Underwood's real killer might get away. This idea plagued him, and you knew all too well that given time White would lose his nerve and confess who he really saw that night. You could not have that," Bainbridge continued calmly. "Jimmy Black scares you, as he scared Underwood. You wanted no one to connect him to Underwood's death, because if that was to occur you feared a backlash on yourself. So, you kept quiet and you insisted the others kept quiet, threatening them along the way."

Stokes clamped his lips together as if he feared what might slip out.

"Unfortunately, White walked in a different world to you and he did not see things the same way. He had to be silenced. The solution was to make it appear he had an accident while drinking due to his sorrow and grief for Underwood. Had you thought about things further, you might have realised the inconsistencies in the plan. However, it fooled many," Bainbridge waited for a response.

Stokes was toying with the door in his hand, considering slamming it closed.

"I hear a lot of speculation," Stokes said, surprising them with his knowledge of such a long word. "I don't hear how it concerns me."

"It concerns you, Stokes, because you murdered White. You got him drunk enough to pass out, not so hard as he was no longer a regular drinker, and then you splashed alcohol about his front room and made sure his pipe was freshly filled with tobacco and alight before you dropped that on the rug. The fire started well enough and you nipped out the back way to avoid being seen. White would have died sooner had not I and my niece happened by."

"Interfering busybodies," Stokes hissed at them.

"The question is," Bainbridge went on, "what are we going to do with this information?"

Stokes waited; his lip curled.

"I could go to the police and reveal White's deathbed

confession, and have you arrested and tried for murder," Bainbridge elaborated for the benefit of Stokes.

Once again, the man curled his lip and glared.

"Or we could come to an arrangement," Bainbridge pressed on.

"An arrangement?" Stokes could barely squeeze out the words, his throat was so constricted with anxiety and outrage.

"I want you to tell the police who sent that violent message to Underwood and why."

"You want me to get Franklin off the hook," Stokes smiled without humour.

"Yes. Quite simply, that is what I want."

"You don't know what you are asking," Stokes started to close the door.

Bainbridge jumped forward before he could do so, placing himself precariously on the threshold.

"I know that there is a big difference between being tried for murder and being tried for obstructing a police investigation. Namely, the death sentence."

Stokes hesitated.

It was enough.

"If you tell the police the truth, I shall not go to them with the information I have from White. You shall not face a murder trial and risk the noose. Jimmy Black will be dealt with by the police for orchestrating the assault on Underwood which resulted in murder."

"You make it all sound so simple and reasonable."

"Is it not?"

"No!" Stokes was gripping the edge of the door tightly. "You don't know Jimmy."

"No, but I do know the difference between the hangman's noose and a short prison sentence. I also know which I would prefer."

Stokes suddenly clasped his head in his hands and stormed back into the room. He paced up and down, his frustration obvious, as he tried to consider his options. Bainbridge was hopeful he had laid things out in a suitable fashion so that Stokes would realise there was only one solution.

The man paced and paced, then he turned around.

"Jimmy Black could get me in prison!"

"Still, it is a better chance than facing the hangman," Bainbridge said calmly.

Stokes paced some more then he growled to himself.

"You have me over a barrel!!"

"What then, is your decision?"

Stokes dug his fingers into his flesh.

"Over a barrel," he hissed to himself. "Very well! Seeing as I am going to be stewed for something, at least I can get back at Jimmy Black. Yes, he was the one who arranged the murder of Underwood. He sent Archie Gubbins to do his dirty work, but his message could not have come from anyone else."

"Why was he angry with Underwood?" Bainbridge asked.

"So, you don't know that?" Stokes sneered. "It was all to do with that stupid boxing match arranged between Simon and Duncan Head. Jimmy Black had placed a large bet on Duncan to win. He was concerned that Simon would win the match and he could not see that happen."

"Duncan said Black was his biggest supporter," Victoria reminded her uncle.

Stokes sighed.

"He was obsessive about it. He had to see Duncan Head win and come out on top. It was more than just the money. It was something deeper and more emotional. When he learned that Simon was to spar against Duncan, he was worried. He knew Simon stood a fair chance of winning and he wanted to place the odds firmly in his favour. He came to us one day and told Simon he had to lose the fight. Simon was reluctant because he had already placed a bet on himself to win and he knew that if he did not do as Charlie Trenchard wanted then his boxing career would be over before it started."

"Truly he was caught between a rock and a hard place,"

Bainbridge said.

"I told him he had no choice, he had to do what Black said, but Simon was anxious about the money and about his future. In the end, he decided to defy Black."

"And he told him that?" Bainbridge said, aghast.

"Simon knew it was either pretend to go along with him and then break his promise during the match and face his wrath afterwards, or refuse to do as Black asked," Stokes explained. "He thought that breaking a promise to Black would be worse than refusing in the first place."

"I understand the complication," Bainbridge said, thinking there had been no easy way for Simon to defy Black. "That is why you are sure Black sent Gubbins."

Stokes laughed softly to himself.

"Black came to me after word got around Simon was dead. He actually had the nerve to pass on his condolences to me," Stokes snorted at the tastelessness of that. "Then he threatened me and told me to say nothing about his involvement with the matter. He was too close to this incident for comfort and he has been worried about it ever since."

Stokes paused thoughtfully.

"I have spent too many hours holed up in this room worrying that someone will realise Black was behind the killing and that he shall retaliate against me. I killed White because of it and ever since I keep thinking what have I become? Murdering my friend to protect the killer of another friend?" Stokes rocked back as the gravity of this hit him. "I owe Simon everything and this was how I repay him? He deserved so much better."

"At least, on that score, you can achieve redemption, for Inspector Dougal is waiting outside and shall listen to your story. Then at least Franklin's life shall not be sacrificed for this charade," Bainbridge told him.

"Do you think he can arrest Black and try him for killing Simon?" Stokes asked hopefully.

Bainbridge gave him a soft smile.

"I jolly well hope so."

~~~*~~~

Events ran smoothly after that. Stokes told his tale to Dougal who at once released Franklin. He sent his men out to arrest Black and charge him with murder. It was going to be a tricky case to prove as Gubbins had been the actual assailant, but if there was a way to have Black found guilty of killing Simon by proxy, he would. In any case, Stokes' confession meant Franklin could go free and that had been the real purpose of the case.

Bainbridge sat down in his favourite armchair with a glass of port and watched the evening sun burnish the sky gold. He was at peace with himself for the moment, a job well done. He was ignoring, as best he could, the nag at the back of his mind that there was one case he had yet to solve. One murder still outstanding. He had a hunch that Houston's murder was going to be one of those cases you whittled away at, rather than raced to a conclusion.

Victoria joined him in the drawing room.

"I have written to mother," she declared, taking a place on the sofa.

"Good," Bainbridge said, then he realised the implication. "Did you tell her you were here?"

"I thought it prudent not to," Victoria reassured him. She leaned back on the sofa. "I know I have a lot to learn Julius, but might I have proven myself worthy of being your assistant in this detective business?"

Bainbridge opened his mouth; his first response was to suggest she go home and forget about being a detective. Somehow that did not come out. It was the responsible thing to do to send her home. Bainbridge hated being responsible.

"I think you have," he said instead. "And you are welcome to stick it out and see where this affair takes you."

He raised his glass to her. Victoria smiled.

"To new adventures," she said.

"To not retiring," Bainbridge added.

Then he poured her out a small glass of port so they could seal the toast. Victoria tasted her drink and endeavoured not to cringe at the sickly sweetness. She was relieved Bainbridge had agreed to her staying, she was not sure what she would have done had he not. She was also considering him, his behaviour the other night had troubled her.

She would ask him about that at some time.

Not just then, though.

Not just then.

We hope you enjoyed this book. You might also like

Memories of the Dead
by
Evelyn James

Brighton 1920.
Clara Fitzgerald is trying to earn a little respect as a female private detective when Mrs Wilton turns up on her doorstep one snowy day. Mrs Wilton has been convinced by an unscrupulous clairvoyant that her dead husband is trying to make contact via strange riddles that supposedly lead to hidden treasure. Clara is quickly on the case to prove the notorious clairvoyant, Mrs Greengage, is nothing more than a scam-artist, extorting money from Mrs Wilton.

But after an unpleasant seance, Mrs Greengage is found with a bullet in her chest and Clara is rapidly a suspect as one of the last people to see her alive.

There is no option but to unravel the mystery for herself, taking on the biggest case of her life.

Available in paperback on Amazon, also on Kindle and Audible

**Red Raven Publications
was founded to bring great stories to
life through digital and traditional
publishing.**

**The majority of our books are
exclusively published through Amazon.
For more information on our titles,
authors, and forthcoming releases,
go to our website!**

www.redravenpublications.com

or find us at
Facebook.com/RedRavenPublications

Printed in Great Britain
by Amazon

23303577R00131